MW00345905

NOT ME

(A Camille Grace FBI Suspense Thriller—Book 1)

Kate Bold

Kate Bold

Debut author Kate Bold is author of the ALEXA CHASE SUSPENSE THRILLER series, comprising six books (and counting); the ASHLEY HOPE SUSPENSE THRILLER series, comprising six books (and counting); and the CAMILLE GRACE FBI SUSPENSE THRILLER series, comprising three books (and counting).

An avid reader and lifelong fan of the mystery and thriller genres, Kate loves to hear from you, so please feel free to visit www.kateboldauthor.com to learn more and stay in touch.

BOOKS BY KATE BOLD

ALEXA CHASE SUSPENSE THRILLER
THE KILLING GAME (Book #1)
THE KILLING TIDE (Book #2)
THE KILLING HOUR (Book #3)
THE KILLING POINT (Book #4)
THE KILLING FOG (Book #5)
THE KILLING PLACE (Book #6)

ASHLEY HOPE SUSPENSE THRILLER
LET ME GO (Book #1)
LET ME OUT (Book #2)
LET ME LIVE (Book #3)
LET ME BREATHE (Book #4)
LET ME FORGET (Book #5)
LET ME ESCAPE (Book #6)

CAMILLE GRACE FBI SUSPENSE THRILLER
NOT ME (Book #1)
NOT NOW (Book #2)
NOT WELL (Book #3)

PROLOGUE

Victoria walked down the streets of New Orleans, gripping her jacket closely to ward of the early morning chill. She was trying not to think of the noise she kept hearing behind her. She'd put it out of her mind at first, maybe just a stray dog or people walking past down another street.

She checked over her shoulder one more time: still nothing.

It had become too late in the night. She'd told her friends she'd wanted to leave that bar earlier, but no one had listened, and in typical fashion, they'd decided to part ways with her at the last second and leave her to walk home alone.

It had seemed like a decent idea at first but in the darkness, passing multiple alleyways and shrouded buildings, she was starting to have second thoughts. She made a mental note to start carrying pepper spray in her purse. It was something she'd always intended to do but never quite got around to.

There it was again. The noise.

With thoughts of pepper spray in her head, it sounded more ominous now.

She walked faster, hoping she could get home before she discovered what was making those noises.

When the noise came again, she glanced back. Was that a person she saw? The shape of a head, the rounded of shapes of shoulders on either side.

Yes, it was definitely a person. They were still a good distance behind her, but he was *there.*

But even so…was he following her? It was hard to tell. The figure wasn't exactly lurking, but he seemed to have no real reason for being there. Just sort of loitering.

His footsteps behind her were coming faster. She didn't dare look back as paranoia sank its hooks. *Besides,* she thought. *How do I know it's a* him?

She picked up her pace. Running was going to be impossible in the high heels she was wearing. Besides, it was probably nothing, and she'd only make a fool of herself. Jesus, she needed to get a grip. That's what she got, she supposed, for leaving the bar so late.

She walked on, trying to ignore him—*the figure*. And though she tried to stay calm, she realized thirty seconds later that she could hear him breathing now. They were close enough for her to think that maybe she *was* being followed.

Victoria threw off her shoes and ran. She was more than a block away from her apartment and she knew she was pretty fast. Even if she did look stupid to anyone that might see her, she didn't care. She ran.

She was gasping for air by the time she reached the porch of her house. She fumbled for her keys, eventually finding them in her purse and stumbling to get them into the lock. She turned the knob and went inside, locking the door behind her, and letting out a sigh of relief.

She was safe. Home. But for some reason, she still didn't feel safe. She couldn't help it. She had to see. Had the guy followed her all the way home? Was he outside, looking at her house from the sidewalk?

She had to know.

Slowly, tentatively, she went to the window and peered outside. Right away, a gasp crawled up her throat.

There was a man out there, his face mostly covered in night shadows. And worst of all, he was not on the sidewalk, but in her yard. In fact, he was staring right at her through the window.

She felt her chest go cold, paralyzed with fear. On the other side of the glass, he offered her a wide, jagged smile. He then raised his hand and she immediately saw the brick he held in his grasp.

Before she could react, he launched the brick in her direction. The window shattered and she jumped back with a squeal as shards of glass came raining down, inside, on the floor.

Then, as if she had a front row seat to an actual, living nightmare, he punched the glass around the frame away and stepped through. He entered her house as if it were the most natural thing in the world.

"Please," she whispered to the stranger, "please. I—I don't want to die."

Victoria was too frightened to say anything else. She found it too hard to draw a whole breath. The man grabbed her face and Victoria swatted at him, trying to kick him away. The intruder managed to get a hand across her mouth and held her tightly to his body.

He said nothing to her, but studied her face as if looking for something very specific. His smile remained on his face as he leaned in close.

She saw him pull something out of his jacket pocket, but she couldn't see it clearly from the angle he held her in. Was that a needle? A pin of some kind?

She couldn't tell. All she knew was that it gleamed in the streetlight that came in through her window.

Victoria screamed against the man's hand as something sharp pricked her. She tried to scream again, but the breath had been taken from her.

And all that was left was darkness.

CHAPTER ONE

FBI Special Agent Camille Grace entered the cell block of the maximum security prison, her body tightening before the familiar sound of metal slamming behind her could rattle her.

She had been to prisons like this many times but that sound still chilled her every single time. It reminded her too much of her past, her youth. Of visiting her own father in a prison very much like this one.

Camille walked down the corridor, accompanied by two guards, towering over her, and tried to stay focused. The serial killer she was about to visit would pry at any weakness of hers, any distraction at all. And she needed to be on her guard. She'd nailed the bastard after all this time, and she was not going to give him any sort of upper hand here.

She couldn't falter here. She needed answers. She had just caught this monster, the only FBI agent who was able to, after a horrific streak of killings. Her name was in newspapers right now and she hated it. She wondered if the killer was aware of this, too.

Putting him behind bars had not been enough. Even with him in custody and off of the streets, Camile was having trouble sleeping. She needed to know *why*. *Why* he had done those wretched things? It tugged at her, like a living thing, the lack of resolution of it all. The seeming meaninglessness of it all. She didn't quite understand it, and that was foreign to her. She'd always been able to pinpoint the motivation and drive of a killer. She'd put numerous killers away in the past. But this one...this one had stumped her. And it was going to drive her crazy if she wasn't able to dig a bit deeper.

Why is it bothering me so badly? she wondered as she made her way down the prison's central corridor.

You know why, she told herself. *This was depraved. This man is sick in a way you've never experienced. You want to know there's a reason—not just that this man lost his mind. This is the first one that hasn't made even a crumb of sense to you.*

Another cell door slammed open, and the guards, as if scared, waited there, and gestured for Camille to walk in while they waited outside.

They were right to be scared, Camille thought. And they didn't even know what he was capable of, as she did.

She entered slowly, not sure what to expect. There, sitting chained to a metal chair, smirking up at her, was Richard. Or, rather, *Sir Richard,* as the press had dubbed him. The most diabolical killer the nation had seen in years. Twenty women in twenty days. He was wearing white pants and a white shirt, with a white bracelet at his wrist. Even in that outfit and in the confines of a prison, he looked evil.

He smiled at her.

"Sit, Agent Grace," he said graciously, gesturing to the chair before him. "I've been expecting you."

God, he chilled her. She clenched her teeth to make sure she didn't say anything untoward. When she did take a seat, she finally allowed herself to offer the simplest of statements. "I'm here to ask you questions."

He chuckled. "Ah, yes, questions. Questions are important. They lead to answers. It's the journey, not the end point. And I am all about the journey."

Camille frowned. There was something off about this man. His eyes had a twinkle in them, but she couldn't tell if it was madness or something else. She stared at him and hoped he was done with his little riddles, his almost pretentious way of speaking, and waited for him to speak.

"We must earn our conversations, Camille," he said. "You know, like a dance. You ask a question, and I must ask you a question. Then you have to ask me a question."

"I'm not dancing with you, Richard," she said, flatly.

"Let's talk, then. Get to know each other."

"What if I don't want to get to know you?"

"Ah, darling, then why are you even here?" The words poured from his mouth like a song. "What we do is talk. You and I are going to talk to each other. I'm sure you have a lot of questions, and I have a lot of answers. I trust you, Agent Grace, to bear the horror of those answers. You have seen the murders I have committed. You have seen the horrors done to those poor souls. You, as a woman, know what it is to feel violated in your very own body. And you know what it is like to struggle against that violation. You know what it is like to wish with all your might to die, to have no more of this, of your own body, the one that took you."

5

He was in a white prison uniform, chain-smoking a cigarette in his hand. As if he didn't already have enough to answer for.

"Do you want to know why I killed those women?" he asked her, trying to sound friendly. "That's why you're here, right?"

"I'm here to find out why," she said, trying to keep him on point.

He smiled again. "I'm not going to tell you, of course. But you will find out, Agent Grace. And in the end, you'll thank me. The nation thanks me."

She grimaced. "What makes you think I'll thank you for anything?"

"You will, Agent Grace," he said. His voice was low, the way it always was when he spoke to her, always seeming to know that she was vulnerable in her youth and innocence. "This is something you're just going to have to trust me on."

"Why did you target those particular women? Were you threatened by them?"

"No, Agent Grace," he said, practically beaming at her now. "It was simply because they were so pretty. So innocent. They deserved to be immortalized. I wanted to capture their beauty forever."

"Why didn't you simply paint them then?" she asked, unable to keep her sarcasm and anger away. The paint supplies in his basement had been the talk of many articles written about him, namely because they'd never seen the fruits of the supplies. It appeared he'd been ready to paint something but had decided against it.

"Oh, I tried that," he said, "But it wasn't good enough. So I painted them in blood. And cut them up, as you know."

"Why?" she asked softly.

"Because I could," he said. "Because I was angry with them. Because I was sad. Because life is difficult. Because it made me happy. It's hard to explain, Agent Grace, but also quite simple."

Camille felt bile rising in her throat. "You're sick," she hissed.

"That is a matter of opinion," he said with a chuckle.

He looked her up and down and she could feel his stare on her. She fought down the bile, doing her best not to lose her composure. But it was harder than she was used to. Richard was an expert at getting in the minds of women and men alike, and making them play his game.

Camille thought about that. And the more she did, the more an understanding came to her. Sir Richard wasn't *only* a diabolical killer. Such a label was almost dangerous. No, he was just a man. Another pathetic, weak man who had been abused as a child. She had always known that; she'd known that from early on in the case. But she had never, until this moment, realized how weak he really was.

She stood, having gotten what she came for. He'd had no real reason. The man was simply outside of his mind. It made her fear what his trial might look like. If he was released and sent to a mental institution, she'd consider it all a failure.

"We're done," she said to him.

He smiled. "Far from it, Agent Grace. As you will soon see."

"Are you threatening me?" she asked, incredulous.

"Threatening you? Oh no, my dear," he said. "I am protecting you."

Many retorts were ready on her tongue, but she swallowed them down. Instead, she turned to the guards behind her. "I'm done here."

She turned her back on him and although she did not see him smile, she could feel it, just as she could feel his stare. It cut through the tension of the room like a blade. She felt his gaze on her until she made it back to her car and as she thought of the fight that was likely waiting for her back home, she wasn't really even sure she wanted to leave.

What was the point of a home if you never wanted to return to it?

It was a question that stung her in more ways than one. It pulled up the ghost-image of her father's face—not the sort of face she wanted to see moments after speaking with Sir Richard.

After all, her father had dominated her life from afar, via memory, for long enough.

Why give him that power now?

Feeling an overwhelming sense of foreboding, Camille started the car and headed home, having a sinking feeling that she was heading right into a break-up.

CHAPTER TWO

She couldn't shake the icy feeling until she returned home. It was a small apartment in downtown Birmingham, Alabama, a place she'd called home for six years now. When she stepped inside, she'd been hoping to smell something cooking. Maybe some salmon or seasoned chicken. Her boyfriend of two years was honestly not good for much; but good Lord, could the boy ever cook.

Plus, it was his day to cook. It was a tradition he'd been failing on lately, but she'd chosen to stay quiet on it.

But there was nothing. The only smell in the apartment was the scented candle, burning on the coffee table. Mahogany. Maybe teakwood. She wasn't sure. Sitting on the couch behind the coffee table was Declan. He was lounged out, scrolling through his phone. The television, mounted on the wall, was showing one of those awful cooking competitions.

"Hey," Camille said, doing her best to fight the irritation she felt rising up.

"Hey, babe," Declan said. He didn't even look up from his phone. As she passed by him, she saw that he was looking through his stock market app. Several months ago, he'd made a risky bet and put a grand or so into a start-up business that had taken off. It had earned Declan almost nineteen thousand dollars in a month.

But then he'd lost it all just as quickly by making other risky moves, moves that had not paid off. And because he was between jobs, he spent a lot of is time doing nothing. Camille came home to this sight a lot. She was really starting to get tired of it.

"No dinner?" Camille asked.

"No, babe. I figured I didn't know what you wanted so it was no used in getting started."

"You could have texted me."

"I know, but I...shit. Is this going to be one of your little miniature blow-ups?" He put his phone down, rolled his eyes, and said, "I really don't want to fight."

"Yeah, me neither." Camille said as she tossed her briefcase down by the kitchen table. She marched to the fridge to see what she could make quickly for herself.

"Then let's not. Did you have a bad day or something?"

"It was fine," she snapped. "How about you? Lots of sitting around, staring at a screen as you play the big-boy lottery?"

"Jesus. Tone it down. No need to be a bitch about it."

The use of *bitch* was a trigger word for her, and he knew it. He always *said* he didn't want to fight, but she thought he rather enjoyed it. Sometimes, she did, too. It was often the most emotion they ever put into anything.

She hated to admit it, but it was true. And after looking into the eyes of a madman today—a madman that came off as civil and almost respectable behind closed doors—it made the context of this relationship seemed trivial. Almost foolish.

"This is a waste of time, Declan."

"What   is?

"This. You and me, trying to pretend we're going to make it work."

"Just because I don't have a traditional job?"

"No. Not only that. It's because we make each other absolutely miserable. And I think we've gotten too used to it. We've become comfortable in resenting one another."

"Resenting?"

"Be honest," she said, leaning tiredly against the kitchen counter. "You resent my job just as much as I resent you for not having one."

Silence filled the apartment. It felt odd to have gone so deep so quickly. Had she really only been home for five minutes?

"I really don't know what you expect of me," Declan finally said.

"I don't expect anything of you. I haven't for a while, and I think that's the problem."

He looked hurt by it, but his eyes drifted back to the TV, as if he were already trying to forget the conversation had even happened at all.

Camille turned her attention to the fridge, in search of something to eat. The fridge was pretty empty. There was some leftover pasta and a jar of salsa. She could make some sort of quick pasta dish but she was in the mood for something lighter. She had a couple of Lean Cuisines in her freezer, too.

She pulled one out and threw it into the microwave to cook.

9

"Do you want to go out to dinner or something?" Declan asked. He asked it in a monotone voice. It was clear that going out was the last thing he wanted to do; he was just trying to fill the silence.

"No. No, I really don't," she said. And she decided right then and there, in that moment, that their relationship was over. The realization was a relief rather than a heartbreak and that, she supposed, told her all she needed to know.

Declan sighed, a sound she had gotten very tired of over the last few weeks.

"Sometimes, I feel like I can't do anything right with you," he said.

"That's not true."

"It is true. I mean, you're always bossing me around."

"I'm not bossy," Camille snapped. "I'd just like to see my twenty-nine-year-old boyfriend show some initiative. Send out some resumes, use those contacts I know your father has been texting you. Stop relying on your girlfriend to make sure you have a roof over your head. Just...*try,* Declan, Try to get a real job."

"Like yours?" he snapped. "A job that keeps you running around all over the place and coming in at all hours of the day and night?"

The microwave beeped, saving her from the conversation. "So good of you to notice when I come in," she snapped right back. She took her lukewarm dinner out of the microwave and carefully peeled the lid back.

"Sometimes I don't even know why you come back at all," he said. She could hear the same realization in his voice. He wanted out just as badly as she did. Why the hell had they kept trudging along for so long, knowing they were going to fail. Were they both that desperate for love and companionship?

"Maybe tomorrow, I won't," she said softly. "And I don't mean that as an insult or jab. Declan...we can't do this. It's ridiculous. Both of us...we're wasting out time."

He said nothing. He simply gave a curt nod. She could not tell if he was hurt or simply had nothing to say. But she could feel the ending of their relationship in the air, like bad news delivered in a doctor's office. Heavy and pressing...stale.

Without another word spoken between them, Camille took her sad little dinner into the bedroom and remained there for the rest of the night.

***

Sometime after midnight, she had the sort of nightmare where she knew without a doubt it wasn't real...just a very bad dream. But it did not make the nightmare any less horrific.

She was walking down a very long, dark corridor. There were jail cells on both sides of her. She was wearing a long pajama gown from her childhood, the one with the frolicking puppy in the field of flowers.

Her feet were bare and she was tracking something down the hall. What was that? Was it blood? Her feet were not cut or bleeding, but somehow, there was blood on the bottoms of them. She left little prints on the concrete floor as she continued through the corridor.

Shapes lurked in the darkness behind the cell bars. Some, she knew, were men. Others had impossible outlines, amorphous shapes that could not settle on a single form. She heard groans and grunts, she heard weeping and the gnashing of teeth.

Form up ahead in the darkness, someone called her name.

"Camille. Oh, my poor Camille..."

It was her father, and there was lunacy in his voice.

She looked back to the floor and now saw that she was walking in blood, not just trailing it behind her. Something moved through it, something dark and serpentine.

"Daddy?" she called.

"My poor, sweet Camille, I'm so sorry. Why did you do it?"

She followed the voice and closed in on the final cell along the hall. She peered inside and though she could not see him, she knew her father was there.

"Do what, Daddy?"

"Haven't you heard of the slaughterhouse?" he asked. "Haven't you seen the dead hogs?"

"Daddy, I'm sorry. I couldn't do it. Please forgive me." Even in the dream, she could hear the hogs squealing, the grunting and the panic. She thought of the pig pen, of the mess along the ground and how she'd tried so hard to avoid it. But he'd insisted that she climb over that fence, and that changed everything.

"No, Camille. I forgive you. I know what you are now...what you've become. I miss you so much. I miss our games. You were my best little girl."

"Daddy, I miss you too."

"Oh, Camille. My little girl," he said. "Why did you have to be so good?"

His voice was growing thicker, his presence drawing close. But she didn't want to see him. She was afraid of what he might look like.

"Daddy?"

"You never got in trouble, Camille. Never. Not once. Not ever. You never made a mistake. I wish you had. I wish you'd had it in you back then."

"I couldn't, Daddy, I'm sorry."

"She hurt my little girl. She hurt you. And when I got my hands on her, I just couldn't stop."

A frail, pale arm rocketed out from between the bars and grabbed her throat. "There you are, my Camille..."

And there were his eyes, hollows of madness lurking in the darkness. He smiled at her and all the blood and—

She was yanked out of the nightmare by the sound of her phone dinging at her. She slapped for it, her hand landing in the empty Lean Cuisine box from dinner and knocking it to the floor. She grabbed the phone and saw the time and the text she'd received.

It was 3:45 in the morning. The text was from Milton, her director at the bureau. And if Milton was texting, it was serious. She sat up on the edge of the bed and gathered her thoughts for a moment, barely aware of the sleeping shape on the other side of the bed.

She only even thought of him when he let out a sleepy remark as she made her way into the bathroom.

"And off she goes again," he said.

She bit back the comment that rose quickly to her lips. She was better than that—and she had to prove it to herself.

Not returning tomorrow would be her response. She'd come back sometime later to get her things, but for right now, her job called. And her job, as sad as it seemed, had treated her far better than the man occupying the other side of the bed over the years.

She left him behind, closing the bathroom door, shutting him out of her life.

CHAPTER THREE

Camille stepped into Director Milton's dimly lit office just shy of five o' clock in the morning. He was the only person there, sitting behind his desk and he looked perfectly awake and alert. She often wondered if the man ever slept.

"Thanks for coming in so early," Milton said. He nodded to the chairs across from his desk. "Have a seat."

She did as he asked, trying to get a gauge on him. He didn't seem worried, but there was an underlying sense of urgency to his posture and the way he looked at her. His hazel eyes were always searching as if trying to read the mind of the person he was speaking with. His brown hair, going slightly gray along the temples, was ruffled and out of sorts, meaning he had been running his hands through it compulsively—something he did when he was nervous.

"I'm not going to lie," Camille said. "When you didn't send any details with the text to come in, I assumed this one was a little murky."

"I wouldn't say 'murky.' But there's a case down in New Orleans that has some dark tinges to it."

"New Orleans?" Even the thought of the city and the surrounding areas made her guts clench up.

"I know it's where you grew up and the memories aren't all the best. But your familiarity with the area and some of the culture would be a huge help."

"Which type of culture?" she asked. She meant that flippantly, almost sarcastically, but Milton's face remained solid and serious.

"Creole." He sighed, shrugged, and added, "Maybe voodoo."

The chills that ran through her were a surprise. The idea of voodoo practices had always unnerved her, mainly because she'd lived nearby several communities that had practiced it. She wasn't sure if there was actual power in it, but the idea of it alone was enough to keep her on edge, feeling uncertain and uneasy.

"What's the case?" she asked, trying to push that bit of fear away.

"At least two murders that we know of. Maybe more. I'd really like for you to be on the road within the hour."

Camille sighed too, but for different reasons. Her heart was racing at the mere thought of returning to the place where she'd grown up.

"I don't know how much use I'll be," she said quietly.

"You'll be working with another agent once you get down there. An agent out of the New Orleans field office. Just new to the area, I think."

"Doesn't matter. I just don't think it's a good fit."

"Why's that?" There was an edge of irritation to his voice, one she'd heard many times but never directed at her.

She wasn't sure how to explain it, especially to someone like Milton. He was used to being surrounded by agents who jumped through even the highest of hoops he set out for them. She'd always been among their numbers, too, but this was different.

"I don't do New Orleans anymore," she said. "And I don't do voodoo."

"Then a little field trip to your childhood home will be just the thing to get you back on track. You're from a small town just outside of New Orleans, right? Upping?"

"Right. I just don't know if..."

She stopped here, trailing off.

"I understand your hesitation," Milton said.

"I don't think you do." But then she thought of Declan and the time she'd wasted with him, of her childhood and how she'd let the horrors she'd experienced define her. Those horrors, though far in her past, were still real enough to her to creep up as she sat in Milton's office. She saw her father's dark, expressionless eyes looking down on her. The splatters of blood on his hands. Her dream came rushing back quickly, as if it had followed her from the apartment and into this office.

"Daddy, I'm sorry. I couldn't do it. Please forgive me."

"No, Camille. I forgive you. I know what you are now...what you've become. I miss you so much. I miss our games. You were my best little girl."

"Daddy, I miss you too."

"Oh, Camille. My little girl. Why did you have to be so good?"

To hell with all of that. She was done running from her past.

She got to her feet a bit more confidently than she'd intended. "Fine. I'll do it. Can you send me the details?"

Milton nodded appreciatively from behind his desk. "You'll have them by the time you get on the plane."

"Plane? It's not that far, sir? I can drive."

14

"No. This one feels urgent. If the press gets wind of it before it's solved, there's going to be a circus down there. I'll have my assistant book your flight. I've already checked. The first one departs for New Orleans in just under two hours."

What this implied but went unsaid was: *There's no time to waste. Move your ass.*

So that's exactly what she did.

She hurried out of his office, leaving Declan and her present behind while her past waited just a plane ride away.

***

Milton was true to his word. As she waited to board her plane, she was emailed the specifics of the case. She started reading them over but was interrupted when she was called to board. With a single overnight bag packed and tossed over her shoulder (a spare she kept in her small office back at the field office), she boarded the plane, reading over the case details. Two bodies, discovered in the woods, just gruesome and staged enough to appear as if they had been used in some sort of occult ritual.

The victims so far had both been women in their twenties. And the latest had a been a singer for a jazz band.

Just like her sister. Just like the sister that had gone missing almost eight years ago and had been presumed dead ever since.

Jesus, how was she supposed to get through this. She hated to think such a thing but the similarities were too much; it made her feel like Upping, Louisiana, and the very large, gloomy shadow of New Orleans was calling her back home. Worse than that, Milton was allowing it and actually sending her there.

She settled into her seat, looking out to the slowly approaching dawn across the tarmac. An image of Nanette's face popped into her head. Nannette, her sister, who had always been able to belt out any note needed to nail a performance. Nanette, who had always been the true apple of their father's eye.

Nanette was gone now, and Camille could accept it on most days. But this morning, as she looked out of the plane window and to the gathering light of a new day, her sister's face remained constant in her mind.

It made her even more aware that in driving out to Louisiana, she was not only refusing to run away from her past any longer. No, she

15

was driving headfirst into an army of ghosts and wretched memories that she'd fooled herself into believing she'd been able to escape.

CHAPTER FOUR

Louisiana wasn't typically to Special Agent Scott Palmer's liking, but he had to admit that it had a wide variety of scenery. From Bourbon Street to the swampy backwoods, it had always felt like a state with a personality crisis. Currently, he was located in the middle of those two extremes, walking through a forest that was more like dense scrublands, headed out to the second murder site he'd visited in the past five days.

It was 6:40 in the morning, and it was already getting hot. He felt like an idiot in his bureau suit, especially the jacket. As he approached the slight clearing in the forest where several State policemen were currently at work, he already knew it would be the same set-up as the previous murder. It was more than just the similarity in locations; it came down to the feeling in the air—a buzzing he couldn't hear, but could feel.

The cops had already roped the place off. Yellow tape had been strung from a series of trees, creating a weird oval shape around the clearing in the woods. Palmer showed his badge and ducked beneath the tape.

The girl had been discovered around two in the morning and they hadn't moved the body yet. The forensics guys were over near a pair of elms, looking at something on the ground. Palmer knew that anything out in the woods needed to be handled with extra meticulous care, so extra steps were being taken to not screw up the scene. Still, he hated that the body was still here.

Maye it was for the best, though. Based on the state of the first victim, Palmer had a good idea of what to expect here. He hoped he was wrong, but…well, he was starting to get a sense of these sorts of things.

A large stump sat at the center of the clearing. There were other stumps and scraggly growths of trees around the clearing, too, but the stump demanded your attention. Even without the nude body of a young woman draped over it, the stump grabbed your attention. He stood at the feet of the body and took it in.

An attractive woman, nearly flawless body. Blonde hair. No obvious signs of death from first glance. But he knew what he'd find if he looked closer.

He sighed and called out. "It's been over four hours. How much longer is the body going to be here?"

"We've got transport on the way right now," one of the guys from State PD said. He was standing a good distance away from the clearing, holding a notepad and discussing something with another cop.

"You guys good over there?" he asked in the direction of forensics.

"No. There's nothing here. Nothing apparent, anyway."

Palmer almost said something else, but he heard a faraway noise, coming from the east. It started out as something like a drone but after a few seconds, he could hear a mechanical sort of thumping to it. This clued him in to what the noise was, and he wasn't sure how he felt about it.

It was a helicopter, heading in this direction.

He'd been told there was another agent coming, some woman from Birmingham that was fresh off of a monster case. She was the woman that had finally taken down Sir Richard. Palmer just hoped she didn't come rolling in with a fat head, trying to call the shots. From what his section chief had told him, she'd apparently grown up around here and was intimately familiar with the area.

Big deal, Palmer thought. *So am I.*

He'd been working out of the New Orleans field office for the better part of four years now. He knew the city well and had even grown accustomed to the area surrounding the city—areas like this stretch of forest, for instance.

The arriving agent, Camille Grace, was also said to be something of a genius when it came to getting into the psyche and mindset of killers.

He didn't mind getting the help, but he didn't like that he'd had no choice in it. He was perfectly capable of handling a simple murder case by himself. But he knew the drill. Pretty white women were being killed close to a very popular tourist destination, so the FBI was going to make sure they got their very best on it before things got out of hand.

He pushed all of this out of his mind as he made a slow circuit around the body. No cuts, no bruises, no real signs of a struggle. There was no visual, topical evidence of sexual assault. The only thing that looked remotely messy was the woman's hair. There were a few leaves in it, and a small cluster of pine needles.

Standing on the woman's left side, he looked down to her hip. He was pretty sure what he'd see there and was not let down. He then checked the area between her breasts and another assumption he'd made was proven correct.

"Shit," he said.

The helicopter drew closer, nearly coming to the spot where it would be hovering over the clearing. It stopped and settled down just shy of the clearing, out near an obscured little field just beyond this strip of woods—the same place Palmer had parked to walk to the site.

The cop holding the notebook looked over to Palmer with a slight look of alarm. "One of your friends?"

"Another agent. Never met her before, though."

Palmer thought he saw a relieved look cross the man's face. A second agent on the scene meant the bureau would be handling the case from here on out. It would just take a phone call to make it official.

While he waited for Camille Grace to waltz into the woods, Palmer hunkered down by the stump, looking for any prints or clues forensics might have missed. There was nothing, and he hadn't expected much so he wasn't disappointed. He'd seen this sort of thing once before, but not to this level of professionalism. Maybe it was good that they'd sent Grace in to help.

She appeared faster than he'd expected, no more than five minutes after he'd watched the helicopter descend behind the trees. Palmer's first thought of her was that she looked smaller than he'd expected. She was short, made to look even smaller by the towering trees around her. She wore the same standard bureau get up he'd seen all other women wear—the jacket and pants that damn near looked like a pants suit, but she wore it with ease. She almost made it look casual.

She had a very pretty face that was accentuated by her red hair. She walked along the tiny trail in the woods as if she'd done it countless times before. She paused a moment to take the scene in, spotted Palmer, and walked to the border of the yellow tape.

"I hope you were better informed than I was on this," she said.

"What do you mean?"

"I didn't know I was working with another agent until I was given the assignment. Sort of a last-minute thing."

"Is that going to be a problem?" he asked, trying to sound as non-confrontational as he could.

"Not at all," she said. She gave a tired smile and offered her hand over the tape. "Special Agent Camille Grace."

He took the offered hand and though her skin was delicate and soft, her grip was firm. "Special Agent Scott Palmer. Good to meet you."

Camille peered over the tape and into the clearing. "You mind?"

"Not at all." He lifted the tape for her and watched as she ducked gracefully under it.

He watched her face as she took in the body. She tilted her head, giving the body an uncertain look. "No blood," she said.

"None. Just like the body before it."

He watched as she checked the neck for signs of bruising and then the hair for any signs of blood that may have come through a lacerated or otherwise damaged scalp.

"My director said the bodies were found in clean states," she said. "The other one was just like this?"

"Yes. And…please forgive me for asking, but do you want me to tell you what I—"

"Ah, there we are," Camille said as she looked to the woman's waist. She leaned in closer and then looked up to Palmer. "Did the other body have an injection mark on her waist?"

"She did. If you don't mind me asking, how did you know to check her hips?"

"No blood and her pubic area doesn't seem to have been compromised. So then I looked for signs that there was at least an attempt of sexual assault. In most cases, bruises are found on the back of the neck, the upper back, or the waist. And when saw no bruises, I did see the injection site right there."

"It doesn't really stick out, though," Palmer said.

"It's not my first time looking for injection sites on a body."

"Have you seen this before?"

"No. I've read about it, though," as she said this, she looked all around. She seemed to look past the cops, straight to the trees and the sky. She then reached into her inner jacket pocket and removed a pair of latex gloves. She slipped them on in a way that impressed Palmer because it showed years of experience. It looked almost like a surgeon gloving up, slipping the gloves on like it was a second nature.

"What about between the breasts?" he asked.

She looked there and he was rather proud of himself when she looked surprised. She'd apparently missed this on her first study of the body. She leaned in closely and looked at the small pin pricks.

"These aren't injection marks," she commented.

"Yeah, I know. It almost looks like acupuncture marks, right?"

20

Camille nodded as she eyed the marks with more scrutiny. She then lifted the woman's arms and legs with her gloved hands. She checked the woman's feet and then even slightly parted the victim's lips and peered into her mouth.

"Have you seen the pinprick pattern on her chest before?" she asked.

"Can't say that I have. At first I thought it was a very bad attempt at some kind of branding, but I don't think that's the case."

"The first victim…where was she last seen before she was found dead?" Camille asked.

"Bar hopping around the French Quarter."

"We need to get this woman out of the woods. We need to see if there's alcohol in her. We need to see what she was injected with. Any findings on the first victim?"

"Not yet. The ME has been looking for about two days now and they've turned up nothing."

She considered this again as she turned her eyes back to the sky and the tops of trees. Palmer thought she might be a bit uncomfortable. "Any idea when they're moving the body?"

Palmer hitched a thumb to one of the cops and said, "He says there's someone on the way. So, I'd guess within half an hour."

"And how far away from here is the site the first body was found?"

For a moment, he thought what he had feared was happening. The rapid fire way in which she was asking questions made him feel like he was working for her. But he figured he'd give her the benefit of the doubt. Something was clearly bothering her and she *had* been flown in, after all.

"Not too far. About twenty minutes."

"You mind taking me?"

"No, not at all. You good here?"

Camille took a moment to look around the scene one more time. She finished her scan as her eyes fell back to the woman on the stump. "Yes, I think I am."

"Follow me, then. I'll take you to a scene that looked almost identical to this."

They ducked back under the yellow tape and headed back for the trail. There was a little less than a quarter of a mile to hike back to the field where the cars were parked, and the day continued to grow hot around them.

He looked over to her only once and he still saw that look of uneasiness on her. She looked as if she wasn't comfortable here, like the woods themselves had unnerved her. He knew the word he wanted to use but just thinking it sent a chill through him.

Camille Grace didn't just look uneasy.

She looked haunted.

CHAPTER FIVE

As far as temporary partners went, Camille supposed Scott Palmer was okay. He was a no-nonsense type and he hadn't tried to overstep and assume authority because he had a penis. He was even quick to point out a few landmarks, just to break the silence and tension in the car, on a few occasions.

He's told her the exact truth when they'd left the site of the most recent victim. The location the first victim had been found in was almost identical to the other. They parked Palmer's car on the side of the road and stepped over a ditch out into the woods. After walking through a grove of trees and brush for roughly half a mile, the trees started to ease apart, giving way to what wasn't so much a clearing, but more of a small field that had long ago overgrown.

A fallen tree sat in the center, one dead limb sticking up into the sky as if trying to touch it with gnarled, wooden fingers.

"The first victim was propped up on that," Palmer said, pointing to the tree as they walked toward it.

"Same injection site?"

"The very same. There were the strange pin pricks on the chest, too."

Camille studied the tree closely. She hunkered down so that her eyes were level with the fallen tree and she could see a few stray strands of hair sticking to the bark. She then checked under the tree—or as best as she could without lifting it from the ground—and then looked all around on the ground. The grass here was dry and overgrown. The only trees growing in the area were thin and brittle, not much more than sickly saplings.

"Where do these woods come out?" Camille asked. "If we were to keep walking straight in any direction, where would he end up?"

"Back to the highway if you head west, a small farm about two miles straight ahead, and nothing but forest for about six miles to the east. We're pretty certain the killer carried the body from the road. There were just enough drag marks along the ground on the way between the road and here."

23

"And you said the most recent victim was barhopping the last time she was seen?"

"Yes."

"And what about the first one?"

"Don't know yet. But I do have a meeting set up with two of the victim's friends in two hours."

Camille nodded as she took another slow scan of the forest. It felt familiar in the same way hearing a song for the first time in about decade is familiar; you know the words, you know the beat, but something about it escapes you all the same. She could all but feel her old home and the tainted memories of it, heavy and pressing like an approaching storm.

"You mind if we head that way now?" she asked, wanting to be out of the forest. "Maybe run me through the neighborhood, let me have a look?"

"Yeah, we can do that. As of right now, the only other thing I'm waiting on is call from the ME or the coroner. They're both pretty baffled that they've found nothing in the victim's bloodstream yet."

Camille almost commented on this. She had an idea of what might be going on, but she didn't want to say just yet. She wanted more evidence, more reason to give her a forming theory. Because if she suggested it and she was wrong, she was going to seem a bit nuts.

Less than five minutes after arriving at the site where the first victim had been discovered, Camille and Palmer headed back to the highway. By the time they reached the car and Camille was sitting in the passenger seat, that old remembered song was a bit clearer and a frightened part of her knew that she'd end up back at her old home before this case was done. Not for the case, of course, but to make sure she settled some old ghosts that had refused to leave her alone for so long.

***

When Camille had lived in the area—in the city of Upping, which was just half an hour to the west—she'd never enjoyed coming to the city. Every now and then, when she'd been much younger, she enjoyed the occasional Sunday lunch and then a stroll through some of the tamer parts of the city with her family, but that had been about it.

Nanette, on the other hand, had been a different story. As the older and more adventurous sister, Nanette had wanted to know everything

24

about New Orleans. She'd loved vibe of the place, the celebratory moods of the people and, above all, the music. As early as the age of eight, Nanette Grace had known she wanted to be a jazz and lounge singer.

Thinking of her sister while Palmer drove them through the French Quarter was haunting. She did her very best to ease it out of her mind. With Upping so close by, it felt like an invitation to disaster.

She looked at the strangely familiar buildings and avenues, trying to get into a mindset of interest and curiosity rather than dread. She'd known coming back to the area would alter her mood, but she hadn't expected anything to this level.

As she took it all in, Palmer's phone rang. He answered it and she listened to his one side of the conversation.

"This is Palmer…oh yeah? Okay…and the family? Got it…okay, you just let us know and we'll get on it. Thanks."

He ended the call and tossed the cell phone into the console.

"That was the Sheriff. They got an ID on the newest victim. Victoria Hudson. State PD is contacting family members. They'll get back to us when there's someone viable to talk to."

"What was the other victim's name?"

"Sara Berringer. Twenty-two years old. I've spoken to the friends already, but they were obviously in a state of shock. With this new victim, I don't know how they'll take it…"

Palmer came to an intersection and took a right. Even now, at just 8:40 in the morning, the streets were filling up. There were no bars open just yet, but people were milling about for breakfast and early jumps on the tourist scene.

Palmer pointed to a nondescript building on the right side of the street. It was dark inside and looked solemnly festive on the outside. "That right there is the bar where the second victim was last seen. Victoria Hudson."

"Was she singing that night?"

"No. Just out drinking with friends. From what I gather, the singing thing was because she was part of a small band. Like a hip-hop and jazz fusion thing. I looked it up on YouTube. They were actually pretty good."

She gave him some credit for that, Checking out a band that might be somewhat related to the case was a bit above and beyond.

"Hey, can I ask you something?" Palmer said.

"Sure."

"I know you busted Sir Richard. And I know you're originally from this area. So I—"

"Did you study up on me?" she interrupted.

"No. Not at all. I got a call at three this morning, and my supervisor told me another agent was coming. An agent that was originally from this part of the country. An agent that just closed a huge serial killer case. He held your name from me until the end, like it was this huge reveal." He snickered and shrugged. "I think you're on the cusp of becoming a big deal."

"How do you know I'm not already?" she joked.

"Good point."

They arrived at the place where Palmer had set up the meeting with both of Sara's friends soon after this awkward yet necessary conversation. It was a small coffee shop in a quiet corner of the French Quarter. They arrived there ten minutes early and Palmer seemed genuinely surprised that the girls were also already there. They were sipping from coffees and sharing an order of beignets. They both looked up sheepishly when Camille and Palmer walked in.

Having already met the girls, Palmer took the lead. He led Camille to the table the girls had selected near the back of the shop. Neither of the girls looked particularly pleased to see him, but they shared a mutual look of understanding. This was going to potentially be painful, but it needed to be done.

"Ladies, this is Special Agent Camille Grace. She'll be part of the investigation from here on out. Agent Grace, meet Susan Stern and Makayla Wentz."

Camille nodded politely to both girls. Susan Stern was a very pretty young woman with golden blonde hair and the sort of body that was so perfect it was almost cartoonish. Makayla was also quite pretty, but sitting there, she looked rather plain. It was also apparent that she'd not slept for quite some time.

"Thanks for meeting with us, girls," Palmer said.

"Sure," Susan said. She looked despondent, as if she were carrying an immense guilt in her heart.

"I know this isn't easy," Palmer said, sitting down at the table with them. Camille did the same and thought she noticed the girls stiffening a bit.

"We'll keep it short and sweet if that's okay," Camille added.

Both girls nodded. Palmer looked over to Camille, as if to ask if she wanted to take a shot at the questioning. It was a smart move, as she knew most traumatized women of this age would relate more to a woman and, therefore, maybe open up a bit more.

"Both of you were with Sara the night before she was killed, correct?"

Both girls nodded, neither managing to look at one another or the agents.

"I understand you were out for some drinks. The last bar you were at together, did you leave together?"

"No," Makayla said. "Sara had wanted to leave before we did. She didn't come out and ask us to leave with her, but it was implied."

"Any reason why she chose to leave earlier than you did?"

Makayla looked over to Susan. Susan did not look back but the reddening of her cheeks indicated she knew she was now on the stand, to borrow a phrase.

"I was talking with this guy," Susan said. "This really interesting guy. I wasn't ready to leave."

"But there were no harsh words exchanged between the three of you?"

"No. But it was obvious that Sara was a little peeved."

"I don't blame her for leaving, though," Makayla said. "She'd had a weird, rough night."

"How so?" Scott asked.

"This older dude kept flirting with her. It was sort if innocent and cute at first but then it sort of got out of hand."

"How long did this go on?" Palmer asked.

"I don't know," Susan said. "At least a few hours."

"Tell me what you remember. Was Sara upset about this, or did she try to play it off?"

"Well, she was definitely upset but tried to hide it," Makayla said. "She got more and more upset when this guy came back and he had his friends with him."

"Was the man nice?"

"No," Susan said. "He was a total douchebag. After a while he said he needed to use the bathroom and then he took off with his friends, but then he came back a second time and it was kind of obvious that he just wanted to look at Sara some more."

"How long did this go on?"

"I don't know for sure," Makayla said. "But it seemed like it took him a long time to come back from the bathroom. And when he came back, he was a lot more obvious. Not aggressive, really...just crude. He kept complimenting Sara's tits and she didn't really know how to handle it. She eventually just got fed up and left."

At the mention of the man checking out Sara's breasts, Camille recalled the odd pin pricks in the valley between them as the girl had laid dead and exposed on the stump out in the woods.

Camille had a thought she didn't dare say. *And neither of you bothered walking home with her after that?* She suppose it would be a relevant question, but she wasn't about to kick these poor girls when they were down.

"Can either of you remember seeing that man in the bar after Sara left?" she asked.

"We've talked about that a lot," Susan said. "I don't think I remember seeing him. But then I again, I was distracted by the guy I was talking to."

She stopped here and started to cry. Makayla put an arm around her friend's shoulders and looked up to Camille and Palmer, like they might have answers for them.

"Any chance you girls know this guy's name?"

"No," Makayla said.

"Do you remember seeing him talk to anyone specifically other than Sara?"

Both girls shook their heads in unison.

Palmer opened his mouth to ask a question but, for the second time in about the last hour and a half, he was interrupted by his phone. He checked the ID and answered quickly, turning away from the girls and getting up to take the call in private. He walked over to the corner and spoke quietly for just a few seconds. When he came back to the table, Camille could see the urgency in his posture. She wasn't sure what the call had been about, but it seemed their meeting with Susan and Makayla was going to be cut short.

"Makayla…Susan…thanks again for your time, but we need to get going. If you think of anything at all that you think might help, don't hesitate to call me."

Camille joined him as he hurried to the door. As he opened it for her and let her pass, he said, "That was one of the local deputies. State PD is talking to the family of Victoria Hudson right now. But perhaps more importantly, they also went by Victoria's place—a tiny townhouse about two miles from here. They found evidence of a recent break-in."

This update presented many options, all of which went unspoken as they hurried to Palmer's car and headed to Victoria's townhouse.

CHAPTER SIX

Palmer had driven by Victoria's small townhouse countless times during his time in the city. It was the sort of home you overlooked, a carbon copy of the many that surrounded it—not just on the block on which it sat, but for all residences within the next half mile or so along the street. It was quite different now, of course. Currently, it was roped off with crime scene tape. A single cop stood at the edge of the shallow porch, nodding to Palmer and Camille as they approached.

"The call I got said there's no body," Palmer said. "Is that right?"

"That's right. Looks like a break-in, but I'll be damned if I can see where anything was taken."

Other than Victoria Hudson, maybe, Palmer thought.

Even before approaching the door, the signs of a break-in were apparent. The front window had been smashed in. A gaping, jagged hole looked in on a small living room. He watched as Camille once again slid on her latex gloves and tried the front door. It turned easily in her hand and the door opened with no issue.

Palmer looked back to the cop on the porch as he typed notes into his phone. "Was it already unlocked when you guys got here?"

"Yeah. Nothing's been changed or altered."

They stepped inside to a quiet and mostly tidy home. Right away, the next obvious clue presented itself, right in the center of the living room rug: a brick, lying in the midst of shattered glass.

At first glance, it was a very small, modest house on a street with similar houses. It was nothing special and in need of repairs, which was likely why a young twenty-something woman had been able to afford the rent. Palmer and Camille entered directly into the living room. Some of the broken glass had made it almost to the front door. It sparkled dimly as they took in the rest of the tiny house.

There wasn't much to it. A small kitchen separated the living area from the only bedroom. There were two doors just off the living room, neither large enough to be doors to other rooms. Scott figured one was a closet and the other the bathroom.

He walked into the kitchen. It was small, with the kitchen table in the middle of the room, surrounded by mismatched chairs. The table

30

was stacked with papers, a laptop, a box of cereal. The door that led to the bathroom was open. He peered inside. There was a shower, toilet and a pedestal sink. The sink was unoccupied and dry.

The other door was a mini-closet. There were a few clothes hanging inside and nothing else.

A sound came from the living area as Camille cleared her throat. He turned to see her standing in the living room, just to the left of the front door.

"I don't see anything," she said. "Not a drop of blood, no dirt, not even a sign of a struggle, aside from the brick through the window."

"There's nothing out of sorts back there, either," he said, hitching a thumb over his shoulder. "Nothing obvious, anyway. Maybe forensics will find something."

He moved further back into the living room, watching Camille at work. Only, it really didn't look like work. She looked like a woman that was on Wheel of Fortune, had only been given three letters to a twenty-letter puzzle, but the answer was right there on the tip of her tongue.

"How far would you say it is between here and where Victoria's body was found?" she asked after a few seconds.

"About half an hour, give or take a few minutes."

Without saying anything, Camille nodded and started walking to the back of the house. Palmer sank down on his haunches, looking at the shattered glass and the brick. It seemed pretty cut and dry, really. A man tossed the brick through the window and came inside. He then injected Victoria right in the hip; whatever he'd injected her with had knocked her out—maybe even killed her. He'd then somehow took the body out of the house, onto the street, and loaded it into his car without anyone seeing.

Palmer walked to the window and checked the broken glass. He could see no blood there, either. The window was fairly low to the porch. After breaking the glass, he didn't think a man of even a short stature would have a problem stepping into it, though his pants were likely to snag along some of the shards.

Camille's voice broke him out of his concentration as she came back into the room. "I'm guessing our suspect is going to be somewhere between five-nine and six feet."

"How do you figure?"

She came over and peered out of the window with him. "Any shorter and he's going to snag himself on the glass when he lowered his first leg down. I don't care how strong the seam of his jeans were, that's going to catch if you're a particularly short man. Any taller, and he'd have to bend himself like an accordion to get past that top portion of jagged glass."

Palmer watched as Camille got down on her knees and studied the floor directly beneath the window. She was careful not to place her knees in glass as she eyed the area for any sign of footprints, dirt, or grime.

"Not a damned thing," she said. She got back to her feet and looked out of the window again. Palmer followed her stare and saw that another police car had arrived, hopefully bringing along forensics.

"If it's okay with you," Camille said, "I'd like to see Sara's body. Can you call the coroner and let him know?"

Palmer figured this would likely be the next stop and he supposed it made sense. He figured Victoria's body would also be there by now. It was the next logical step to make.

They exited Victoria's townhouse, leaving the broken glass and the brick for the forensics team. There was a story to be told among all of it and Palmer didn't doubt more of it would be revealed soon.

***

Visiting a coroner's office had never bothered Camille. While she valued human life and hated the idea that losing loved ones was a fact of life, she also understood the need and necessity of funeral homes. Besides that, she'd seen bodies in rough shape more times that she cared to admit.

But when she met with the coroner assigned to this case, a gaunt-looking man named Oswalt, she instantly felt a sense of tension. It didn't help that the medical examiner was also there. The coroner and the ME already having consulted together implied that everyone on this case was equally stumped and working together for answers.

The medical examiner was a short and portly man named O'Toole. His eyeglasses and blank expression made him look a bit like an accountant.

The bodies of the two victims were being held in a private room in the basement of the coroner's office, given the increasing likelihood of a connection between the two. Oswalt led them down the thin stairwell and into the downstairs area; he had a grim look on his face.

"I received the body of Victoria Hudson no more than an hour ago," he said. "I have yet to perform an autopsy on her, but based on the identical presentation of her body to Sara Berringer's, I expect the same results."

"Which are?" Camille asked.

"A lot of nothing."

He led them to the room downstairs and opened the door. There were two examination tables in the room, with stainless steel counters on both sides. What Camille saw on the tables made her hesitate for a moment. She saw Victoria's body fist. It was somehow much more jarring here in the sterile and well-lit confines of the examination room than out in the forest. Sara Berringer was on the table next to her. She was just as good looking, though pale and with sewed up incision marks trailing down her torso.

Camille walked to Sara's left side and looked to her hip. It was a bit harder to see the injection mark being that it was several days old, but it was there. She then looked to the girl's chest. Just above where the incisions had begun, were the same pin prick marks as they'd seen on Victoria.

"Is there anything at all you can tell us?" Camille asked.

"Yes. I'm almost certain it was not the injections that killed these women—though that's admittedly a brave thing for me to say, given that I have no idea what they were injected with. Nothing showed up in Sara's results. Anyway, no, I don't think the injection is what killed them—not Sara, anyway. There's heavy evidence that she may have been suffocated."

"I don't understand." Camille said.

"Think of it like putting a pillow over someone's face," O'Toole chimed in. "When we examine a body that has been smothered or suffocated, we tend to find a few things. First, the lungs tend to be filled with a large amount of air. When someone dies of suffocation, the process of dying is a lot like a person trying to hold back a sneeze. As they're dying, the body is desperate for air, so it will try to inhale every bit it can. So, the lungs are full of air...as was the case here."

"And there was nothing out of the ordinary in her bloodwork?" Camille asked. "Did you find any chemicals that were uncommon?"

"No, nothing out of the ordinary," Oswalt said. He seemed annoyed that he was having to state this again. "No hard drugs, no sedatives,

33

nothing that *should* have knocked her out. Nothing out of the ordinary. This is, of course, assuming Ms. Hudson's results come back the same."

"Any signs of rape or sexual abuse?" Camille asked.

"None that we saw. No traces of semen or other bodily fluids. No wear and tear in the typical places."

That was the final bit of confirmation she needed. She winced, not liking where her mind was headed, but she was quite sure she now had a theory. It was the same one that had come to her earlier, the one she'd tried to ignore. But it was becoming more and more apparent with each new answer—or, rather, lack of an answer

"And that's all we have, really," Oswalt said. "It may not seem like much, but it—"

"No it tells quite a bit," Camille said, crossing her arms and studying the two girls. "The killer followed the victims from areas in the French Quarter. He injected them with something that apparently isn't showing up in bloodwork. He then took their unconscious bodies to places in the woods. And maybe he suffocated them. No blood, no butchering, no sex."

O'Toole nodded slowly. "Yeah, that sums it up."

Camille slowly looked away from the bodies and then eyed both O'Toole and Oswalt. "How often does this happen? A body that's clearly been drugged but nothing pops up in the bloodwork?"

"Not too often," O'Toole said.

"Have you ever seen any neurotoxins that don't show up in bloodwork?"

"That's extremely rare. I think if we…wait. Are you really thinking…shit."

"What?" Palmer said.

Camille sighed. Not only was she going to have to face her theory; she was going to have to speak it out loud. And after that, there was no coming back.

"Agent Palmer…how familiar are you with drugs and methods used in voodoo practices?"

CHAPTER SEVEN

It was approaching noon as they left the coroner's office. Camille was very aware that Palmer was in a different mood now. Some of the poise and confidence he'd showed during the morning was gone. Now he was stumped and having to look at this case from a different angle.

"How did you get to voodoo so quickly?" he asked.

"You're familiar with the area," she said. "You mean to tell me it never crossed your mind?"

"It did for just a second, but I figured there wasn't nearly enough evidence to get there."

"I didn't want to go there, either," she said. "But what other drugs are you aware of that are injected into people, knock them out cold, and don't show up in bloodwork?"

He didn't have to think about it for long, which was good. She really didn't want him diving into a funk and making this already tense case even trickier.

"Well, there are some psychoactive drugs that rarely show up and even if they do, they present oddly. Benzos, for example. And if the girls had been actively drinking before they were injected with some sort of psychoactive drug, it would be possible, I guess. But it would have to be tampered with a bit."

"If it *is* voodoo and it's someone that knows what they're doing, I doubt they'd have an issue with tampering with drugs. There are neurotoxins from certain fish and toads that are highly coveted in serious Haitian strains of voodoo that can do everything we're looking for. They can be *very* tricky to find in typical blood tests just because of the way the human body absorbs and processes them."

"And how, exactly, do you know all of this?"

"I've been here for a year now. You hear things, you get hooked, you read up on stuff."

"I grew up around here," she pointed out. "And I never went through a voodoo phase. Anyway, voodoo or not, there's still a sicko out there that's drugging and then mutilating women. And I'd like to check the bar the first victim visited before she went missing—the one you pointed out earlier."

Palmer nodded and readjusted his course, turning left down a one-way street. It was just a quick ten-minute drive, located on the western rim of what served as the French Quarter. Because it was coming to the end of the lunch rush, the streets and the bars were thickening up. They had to park blocks away from the bar, a refined and minimalist-looking place that was trying hard to be more of a classy lounge than a typical New Orleans bar.

When they entered the bar, Camille was pleased with their timing. It wasn't quite busy yet, though there was a steady hum of activity at the bar. Figuring the bartender would be a good place to start with their questioning, they headed to the bar.

As they sat down at the sleekly polished oak bar, Scott wasted no time in looking over at the taps.

"You gonna get upset if I get a beer?"

"I'm not your boss," Camille said. "I personally never drink while on a case."

Scott lifted his right hand in a little half-salute to get the bartender's attention. She was a thirty-something woman with enough makeup to pull off twenty-five. After delivering two martinis to a man and woman in business suits on the other end of the bar, she came over to them with a smile.

"What can I get'cha?" she asked.

"A beer," Scott said. "Whatever's cheapest for the lunch specials."

"Anything else?"

Camille deftly showed her badge, keeping it low on the bar so as not to attract attention. "We'd like to ask you some questions, too."

"Um...okay. Want me to get the beer first?"

"Yes, please."

The bartender went to the taps where she grabbed two glasses and poured what Camille assumed was a local brew that would probably taste just a bit better than pond water. She brought them over, but her smile was gone now. She looked a little worried, actually.

"So what sort of questions?" she asked.

Palmer took a long sip of his beer, swallowed it down, and wasted no time. "We need to know if you recall anything about a strange man hanging around a young woman five nights ago."

The bartender smiled, as if she was being pranked. "This is a bar in the French Quarter," she scoffed. "I see that about a hundred times a night."

"This guy would have probably stood out," Camille said. "We're looking into the disappearance and subsequent murder of a woman that was last seen here one week ago before her body was found out in the woods."

"Ah shit, yeah, I heard about that. I wasn't here that night, but Courtney was."

"Courtney?"

"Another bartender. She's right over there, actually." She pointed to a woman of about the same age, currently carrying a bottle of wine to a table near the back. The bartender waved her over quickly and Courtney came over. She looked hurried and a little frazzled as she joined the other bartender.

"Courtney, these are FBI agents. They were asking me about that girl that was in here the other night. The one that disappeared."

"Oh," Courtney said. "Oh. Yeah, sure. Sara, right?"

"That's right," Camille said. "You were bartending that night?"

"Yeah. And I didn't know her that well, just enough to know her name, you know? She came in a lot. Usually with friends. Sara Berringer."

"What do you remember about that night?" Scott asked. "We're specifically interested in any men you noticed her talking to."

"There weren't that many that night, which was weird," Courtney said. "She came in around ten with her friends. I did notice that she would sit by herself for a while here and there."

"Was she alone when she came in?" Camille asked.

"I don't remember, honestly. Sorry."

"You said you knew her by name, right?"

"She sometimes had one or two friends with her but yeah, on occasion she'd come in by herself, have a few glasses of wine, and leave.

"Did anyone other than her friends join her that night?" Scott asked.

"Yeah. A guy went over to her during one of those times she was sitting by herself. Sort of distant and nervous, I thought. He just stood there for a minute, talking to her. And then she laughed at something he said. A good laugh. Not, like, a polite one just to get rid of him. And he smiled, and then sat down with her."

"Can you describe the man that she was talking to?" Scott asked. "Was he a local?"

"Hard to tell. He was talking like he was—he had that sort of *Lo'sana* accent. You know? He wasn't dressed fancy or anything, just a tee shirt and jeans. But he had a really thick, well-groomed beard."

"What did she talk to him about? Did she seem nervous, like she was hiding something?" Camille asked.

"I don't know. I don't ever really eavesdrop, you know? I mean, I just saw that he had a beard and weird hair, and he was talking to a girl I slightly recognized. And like I said, she *was* with her friends the majority of the time."

"Did they leave together?" Camille asked. "Sara and the man, I mean."

"No. He left before she did. I figured Sara had shot him down. I'm pretty sure Sara was in here with her friends for at least half an hour after the guy left. Maybe longer. But again...I deal with a lot of people every night, so none of this is exact."

Camille tried to envision the scene in her head. Looking across the bar to where the business-suited folks sat, it was easy to put it together.

"Any chance you know the guy's name?" Scott asked.

"Sorry, no." She paused here, cocked her head and then added: "But hold on..."

She took a few steps over to where the original bartender was now working on a mojito for a new patron. Courtney spoke to the bartender and she nodded a bit. She delivered the drink and then came back over to where Camille and Scott were sitting. Camille took the opportunity to finally start on her beer. One sip in and she realized she really didn't want it.

"So," the first bartender said. "A guy with a sleek beard and this crazy just-got-out-bed hair?"

"Yeah," Courtney said. "That was him."

"Shit," the other bartender said.

"What?" Camille asked.

The bartender took out her phone. Camille watched as she opened up Instagram and started scrolling through her followers. She selected one, brought the account up and then hunted for a picture. She showed it to Courtney with a bit of a frown on her face.

"Is that him?"

"Yes!" Courtney said. "Yeah, that's him."

The bartender showed the picture to Camille and Scott, placing her phone on the bar between them. "His name is Oliver Traylor. I can give you his address. And if you'll let me, I'll even drive the car for you so you can arrest the prick."

"I take it you know him personally?" Camille asked.

"A few hook-ups after my shift. One of those mistakes that's hard to kick, you know?"

"When were you last involved with him?" Palmer asked.

She shrugged. "Maybe four months ago. The scary things is..."

She stopped here, her eyes glossing over a bit. She suddenly looked scared, as if she'd looked into her past and seen a demon staring back.

"What is it?" Scott asked.

"The reason I finally stopped seeing him was because he was getting rough. Dominant. He...uh, well, he started choking me one night. Thought I'd like it. And when I got mad at him, he had this look. I thought he was really going to hurt me."

Camille looked over to Palmer and saw that he had the same feeling she had. He was already getting out of his seat.

Forgetting his beer completely Palmer got to his feet as Camille slid the phone back to the bartender.

"I think we'll take that address."

CHAPTER EIGHT

Camille was rather fascinated with how much more familiar the city started to feel the more she was driven through it. It was nearing 5:00 in the evening as they made their way to the address the bartender had given them, and traffic was getting worse. She did not envy Palmer the task of driving through it.

"Let's hope this Oliver character is one of those work-from-home types," Palmer said from behind the wheel. "I don't know about you, but I really don't want to have to waste more time finding out where he works. I'd *love* to figure this one out before dark."

Camille nodded. She recalled how lively New Orleans got at night—particularly the French Quarter—and though she could see the appeal of it to most people, it was just not for her. Much had changed about the area, but not enough to feel like some new and exciting place that would be different for her.

One thing that had not changed was that the side streets that contained mostly apartments and small, mom-and-pop businesses weren't quite as brightly lit as the central thoroughfares. Oliver Traylor's street was no exception. It was the type of street that allowed parking on both sides, barely enough room for one single lane of traffic to pass through, much less the two that the road allowed.

Being that it was about a mile and a half away from the French Quarter proper, the area was not very crowded. The building was of a simple design, the front adorned with a few shrubs, the side mostly tidied and tagged with the sort of graffiti that looked almost respectable. Though she hated to think in stereotypes, she did start to feel a bit better about the chances of finding Oliver at home. The neighborhood had the feel of software designers, copyright and marketing gurus, maybe brave and opportunistic twenty-somethings starting to dabble in the stock market.

They entered the building and headed to the second floor, as the bartender had indicated that Oliver lived in apartment 205. The hallway was brightly lit thanks to the evening sunlight coming in through large, rectangular windows. From somewhere further down the hall, someone was blaring music. A chunky baseline seemed to thrum through the walls.

"Is it sad that I know this song?" Scott asked as they approached Oliver's door.

Camille took note that it was the first ting he'd said to her that could be considered humorous or conversational. It was a small token, but one that she took as a sign of openness. He was a human being first, and an agent second.

"A bit. But I'm a fan of '80s pop, so I can't judge."

He did not smile, taking the brief moment of light-heartedness to knock on Oliver's door. As they waited, Camille's hand went to her jacket's inner pocket where her badge waited. She quickly glanced down to her holstered Glock, not thinking they'd need it but being reassured by the sight of it.

Ten seconds passed, and there was no answer. Scott knocked again, this time to the same result.

"This *is* New Orleans," Scott said. "Maybe he's out at bars…stalking other women."

Camille turned to face him, her eyes briefly going past him and back down the hall, toward the stairs they'd just come up. When she did, she saw a man she thought might be in his late twenties. He hesitated where he stood, his eyes locked on the two strangers in the middle of his hall. There was a plastic bag in his right hand, a case of beer resting inside of it, and a phone in his left.

The lower half of his face was covered by a well-maintained beard. And though he wore a baseball cap, Camille thought she saw enough of it sticking out of the edges to be considered "crazy hair." More importantly, the alarmed face that stared back at her was the same one she'd seen on the bartender's phone screen just twenty minutes ago.

"Palmer," Camille said, nodding subtly in Oliver Traylor's direction.

Palmer turned and saw him, too. "Oliver Traylor?" he asked.

And that was all it took. As if someone had fired off a marathon gun, Oliver took off running. He dropped the plastic bag, the glass bottles clinking inside, and dashed back in the direction of the stairs.

"Shit," Scott said, taking off right away.

Camille followed, her eyes keeping up with Oliver. He was damned fast and if he got to the stairs, he'd be home free. Camille gave an extra burst of speed, momentarily forgetting that she had a partner in this.

41

Scott was still just ahead of her, but she easily overtook him. She saw Oliver reaching the stairs, taking the first one down.

Camille made it to the stairway a single second after Oliver took his third step down. Grabbing the rickety handrail installed into the wall, Camille leveraged her weight and managed to swing a kick that clipped Oliver in the back of the leg.

He went sprawling down the rest of the stairs, tumbling down to the landing below. He tried his best to get up as quickly as he could but as he steadied himself against the wall, Camille came leaping down the stairs.

She took out her cuffs quickly, working on what she'd always thought of as autopilot. Before Oliver could get his bearings, Camille had the cuffs around his wrists. He did his best to fight but by that time, Scott was also there, pressing him against the wall.

"You ain't got to do that, man," Oliver said. "I ain't gonna cause no trouble."

"Why did you run from us?"

"Two spooky looking strangers were knocking on my door, man! And you guys sure as shit ain't Jehovah's Witnesses. I figure whatever it is, it ain't good news."

"I don't buy it," Scott said.

"We have to ask you some questions," Camille said. "We can do it the easy way and you can invite us back to your apartment, or you can be a moron and make us take you to the station and ask you in an interrogation room."

"This is bullshit!"

"Come on," Palmer said, turning Oliver back towards the steps. "The beer you left in the hallway is getting warm. And the only thing I hate more than having to run after suspects that don't think before they act is a warm beer."

***

"Hold up. You think I *murdered* some chick?"

Oliver sat on his couch, which was littered with game controllers, a laptop, and a fast-food box. He held his hands out in front of him, perched on his legs, as if to make sure to remind Camille and Scott that they'd put him in handcuffs.

42

"What we think is that you were the last person known to have spoken to a woman named Sara Berringer before she was murdered," Camille said.

"Man, I talk to tons of girls every week."

"How often do you talk to girls that are then murdered immediately after you meet with them?"

Oliver had nothing to say to that.

"What did you and Sara talk about?" Palmer asked.

It was obvious that he was trying to remember but was coming up empty. "Look, I don't know. I ask them questions and pretend to listen. All I'm really thinking about is how I'm going to get them back here."

"My God, why?" Palmer asked. "This place is a dump."

"So what did you do when you left the bar?" Camille asked. As she asked him questions, she scanned the apartment for any signs of needles or syringes. Unless they were all hiding under the other mess, she saw none. She also noticed that there were no voodoo artifacts anywhere. Those, too, could be hidden, but Oliver was starting to strike her as the sort of guy that probably spent more time worrying about getting laid than he would anything like voodoo, which took at least some degree of dedication.

"I met up with some friends."

"And what did you and those friends do?"

"We went to a party."

"Where was the party?" Palmer asked.

"A house just off of Esplanade. I remember that because I had to drive there."

"Why is that?" Camille asked.

"Because my friends were already hammered, and I'd only had a few beers. I had them when I spoke to that chick at the bar."

Camille was unable to hold it back any longer. She strode up to him and stared into his eyes. "That *chick* was abducted and murdered. Call her a chick one more time and I'm going to break your nose."

"Okay…okay, sorry."

"Okay," Palmer said. "You drove to the party on Esplanade. Then what?"

"We stayed at the party for a few hours."

"And were your friends with you the whole time?"

"Nah, we split off after a few hours."

"Did you ever see Sara Berringer at the party?"

"You mean the chi...the woman from the bar? No. Never saw her again."

"What about a woman named Victoria?" Palmer asked.

Oliver thought about it for a moment and shrugged. "You mean like my age?"

"Yes. Probably."

"Closest I know is a woman named Vicki. She' a client of mine, but she's closer to fifty."

"What are the names of your friends?"

"Chris, Jeff, and Steve. You can call them right now and they'll back it all up. Shit, man, there are at least twenty people that can vouch for me. There was a karaoke machine and a lot of liquor and I made an ass of myself."

Camille felt the lead slipping away. With that many people and a party, it was going to be very easy for his alibi to stick.

"When you were at the bar, talking to Sara, do you remember seeing any other men? Maybe someone lurking around?"

He shook his head, almost disappointed. "No. I don't really go to those places looking for the dudes, you know?"

Camille looked to Palmer and saw the look of frustration on his face. He returned Camille's gaze and shook his head.

Camille took the cuff key out of her pocket and unclasped them. Oliver flexed his wrists in relief, as if he'd been cuffed for hours when, in fact, it had been no more than twenty minutes.

"And you had no idea that someone you spoke to that night was killed?" Camille asked.

"Not at all." The realization of what that meant sank over him as he looked to his now cuff-less wrists. "Damn, man. I'm really sorry to hear it. Like, for real."

He moved slowly as he reached to the coffee table where he'd set the plastic bag with the case of beer. He tore into the cardboard case and retrieve a bottle, popping the top.

He eyed the agents oddly, nodding to the case. "You guys want one?"

Camille rolled her eyes at him, incredulous. "Goodbye, Mr. Traylor. Thank you for your time."

She turned to make her exit with Palmer but saw that he was already headed for the door. Something was clearly bothering him, though he was not being outright rude. It made her wonder if he was simply not used to working with a partner. If that were the case, she supposed she understood. Besides, who was she to judge? She was wrestling with her own demons, being this close to childhood traumas. There was no way they would successfully work together if they were both struggling.

She followed him out, closing the door to Oliver's apartment—and their only lead so far—behind her.

CHAPTER NINE

He'd always thought the French Quarter during the day was this charming, almost quaint place. But then the night came and it became a dark and brooding place, as if the area were possessed by a demon that lugged only darkness behind it.

That's why he preferred to hunt at night. He liked moving in the darkness. He liked the feeling that no one could really see him. In a city where it was a staple for women to show their tits for some stupid beads, people like him often went unseen. He thought it was the work of that demon, making sure the darker things went unseen.

He was on the hunt, looking for someone that looked like HER. They wouldn't look exactly like her, but a close resemblance would do.

He saw a young woman, walking with two others. She might do. The hair was the same color, she was a bit taller than normal, and her smile was piercing.

Yes, she would do just fine. She might be the one to help bring her back.

A few would have to die along the way. In fact, a few had already died. But he'd known there would be sacrifices and he was fine with that. If you wanted the attention of a woman in this city, all you had to do was pull out a camera or some stupid beads.

He followed them, his eyes on the slightly taller one with the blinding smile. He followed them until they entered a bar and then he waited. He almost decided to go in but kept his distance, watching the door and waiting.

If this was going to work, he had to be patient. There could be no mistakes.

So he waited. He was not sure how long he waited. The darkness of the city mades time an abstract notion.

But then she came out.

He saw the beam of her light illuminate the street, guiding her friends. She saw him, but she didn't know him. She didn't know his pain, the empty place she left in him. She didn't know what she did to him, or why he waits for her.

Ah, but it's not HER. Not really. He'd nearly lost himself there. It's happened a few times. Scary stuff.

He watched her getting closer, saw her start to smile. Her friends had moved on, oblivious to his presence.

Yes, she'll do.

It's now or never.

He began to move.

She crossed the street, waving to a truck that allowed her to pass ahead of traffic.

He felt inside his coat pocket, fingering the plunger end of the syringe.

He started to cross the street but then saw that she'd joined a young man. He wrapped an arm around her and they started walking in the opposite direction.

He followed them until they stopped at another bar.

And again, he has to wait.

But he's done this several times now and is used to it. It has only worked out twice and these times were reminders that the hunting and the waiting were SO worth it.

He was doing this for her. He could have her back.

And if it just took some waiting in the presence of the demon of this city, he was fine with that.

CHAPTER TEN

Even though Camille had not yet met with the family of Sara Berringer, she still felt like she was backtracking when she and Palmer decided to them. She stared aimlessly out of the passenger side window into the freshly-fallen night as Palmer drove. Sara's parents lived on the outskirts of the city, just far enough away from New Orleans to avoid the noise, but still close enough so that their neighborhood still held that rustic New Orleans charm.

"Was the family helpful when you spoke to them the first time?" Camille asked.

"The father was. He was furious and if I would have let him, he would have gone out with a shotgun to find the killer on his own. The mother was a wreck, though. You know how that sudden news sort of makes people fold in on themselves?"

She nodded. Yes, she did. She'd seen it countless times: mothers, fathers, and siblings that seemed to almost implode when faced with the sudden news that someone they loved deeply was dead.

"Thanks for this, by the way," Camille said.

"Thanks for what?"

"Retracing steps you've already taken just because I showed up on the case."

"Oh. It's not a problem. Besides, it's my experience that loved ones are better to question a few days removed from such a loss. They'd have more time to process. The hurt...it's still there but there's a name for it."

Camille understood this, too. And she rather liked the way he'd worded it. At face value, Scott Palmer seemed like an almost generic, run-of-the-mill agent. But she was starting to understand that he was a bit deeper than that. He had a keen sense of the shape of a case and seemed to have a reserved sort of understanding of what it meant to be an effective agent.

They arrived at the Berringer residence fifteen minutes later. It was a gorgeous French-style house in an affluent subdivision—the sort with its own pool, tennis courts, and clubhouse.

Palmer parked at the center of the U-shaped driveway and they walked to the front door, easily seeing their way along thanks to the small decorative lights alongside the brick-rimmed sidewalk.

The door was answered very quickly. Camille wondered if Mr. and Mrs. Berringer had been waiting for someone to visit. Maybe someone with news about their dead daughter. Maybe with news that the monster who had taken their daughter's life had been caught.

The woman that answered the door, presumably Mrs. Berringer, looked worn down and tired. She seemed pleased to see Palmer at first but when she saw a second agent with him, she seemed to understand the situation.

"No news yet, Agent Palmer?" she asked.

"No, ma'am. I'm very sorry. In fact, there's been another murder. Exactly like Sara's. I was really hoping I could talk with you and your husband again."

"Of course," Mrs. Berringer said. Her face tightened as she tried to hide her disappointment. "Come on in."

She led them into a large yet minimally decorated den where a man sat quietly on a leather couch, sipping a tumbler of dark liquor. There was a TV on the wall, but it was not on. The room was quiet, dead silent. He barely even looked up at Camille and Palmer as they entered.

"Jack?" Mrs. Berringer said. "Agent Palmer is back with another agent."

"Agent Grace," Camille said. "Thank you for allowing us in."

"As I was telling Mrs. Berringer," Palmer said, "we were hoping ask some more questions."

"I'd rather not," Jack Berringer said. Camille could hear the anger and hostility in his voice. "I've talked quite enough about Sara over the last few days."

"Sir, there's been another murder," Camille said. "A girl of about the same age, murdered in the exact same way."

This got his attention.

"What?" he asked. The single word was shaky, almost disjointed.

"Another girl was murdered, and we have reason to believe it could be the same killer."

"Who...?" Ms. Berringer asked.

"A young woman named Victoria Hudson," Palmer said. "Does that name ring any bells?"

The aggrieved parents looked to one another and shook their heads. "No," Mr. Berringer said. "Then again, Sara had lots of friends so she could have had a friend by that name and we just wouldn't have known."

"Lots of friends," Camille said. "So she was popular?"

"Somewhat," Mrs. Berringer said. "She was always telling us stories about people she was hanging out with. There were so many, though, that it was hard to keep up with all of them."

"Did you ever hear her talk about people she flat out didn't like?"

"No. Even if there was someone Sara didn't like, I don't think she would have ever said a negative word against anyone."

"Are there any enemies you can think of that she might have had?" Camille asked.

"Palmer already asked us this stuff," Mr. Berringer said. Apparently the anger he'd felt upon learning about his daughter's death had morphed into bitter resentment.

"But no," Mrs. Berringer said. "We don't know of any people that she held grudges against, or vice versa."

"What about family members?" Camille asked.

"Again, no."

"Are you guys about done asking questions?" Mr. Berringer snapped. There was the anger. But it was also punctuated with sadness. Camille could hear it in his voice. One wrong word or thought and the man was going to crack.

"Sir, we are only trying to—"

"Are you—?"

"Look, Agent Grace," he suddenly said, putting his glass down on the coffee table in front of the couch. He got to his feet and the way he swayed made it clear that he'd had a few glasses long before they'd showed up. "I know you're just doing your job and I'm thankful that you and Agent Palmer took the time to come see us again but honestly, we're not going to be able to tell you anything else. Sara's dead and we have no answers. None. So please don't come back to us unless you have answers for us."

Camille could see tears brimming in the corners of his eyes. She hated that they'd pushed him to this point.

"Yes, sir," Palmer said. "We understand."

"Good!" The rage was there, fully present now. Camille knew that it was being directed at them because they were the only tangible things that he had to direct it toward. The killer, as of right now, had no face. But they were standing right there.

50

Camille and Palmer turned to leave. Mrs. Berringer showed them out and mouthed a sad "I'm sorry" to them as they made their way out onto the porch.

Back in the car, Camille and Palmer remained quiet until they reached the end of the driveway.

"Well, that was a waste of a trip," Palmer said.

"Maybe. But now we know she had a wide circle of friends, right? So there should be plenty more people to talk to."

"But none of that is going to be of any use unless we have at least SOME indication of who the killer might be."

Camille could tell that the interaction with the father had sapped some of the confidence out of Palmer.

"Was he even angrier when you first spoke to him?" she asked.

"Yes. His brother was there. They had to restrain him from going to the gun cabinet and heading out on a hunt for the killer."

"My God. Then again, I can't imagine how it must feel to lose a perfectly healthy child so quickly, so unfairly."

Palmer nodded but remained quiet behind the wheel. He didn't speak again for another five minutes and the remark that came out of his mouth surprised her.

"I'm calling it a night. I know you came in fast today and never really got a break. If you don't have a hotel room yet, you're welcome to my couch."

"I appreciate it, but if you can point me in the direction of a rental car place, I'll just snag a hotel. After all, it seems like I'll be in town for at least a few days."

What went unspoken but was clearly communicated in that comment was that she didn't expect the case to be wrapped anytime soon.

What was a little less obvious was the thought that paraded through her head the moment Palmer said he was calling it a night.

Camille had no intention of finding a hotel yet.

She thought she might hit up the French Quarter and do some bar-hopping of her own. This killer was not going to stop at two. The presentation and similarity of the bodies pretty much screamed this fact.

And she thought the best approach for now would be to visit the killer's stomping grounds.

CHAPTER ELEVEN

Tara knew she should call it a night. The martini in front of her really should be her last one. She'd catch a taxi home, probably splitting it with her friends, so that wasn't an issue. But she had church in the morning.

She hated going to church but her mother insisted on it. And now, even at twenty-one years of age, Tara tried too hard to please her mother.

Which was weird because her mother would never approve of her staying out until after midnight to drink with friends.

The thing of it was that she really wasn't drunk. She was barely even buzzed. And when she was paying fifteen bucks a pop for martinis, she felt like she should get *something* out of it.

Maybe a guy. She and her friends never had problems getting guys to swoon over them. And while Tara was not the one-night-stand type, there was nothing wrong with some attention. And maybe some making out back in the darkened corridor that led to the bathrooms.

But the only guy that was showing their group of four any attention right now was a guy wearing a tacky Carhartt cap and steel toed boots. No thanks.

She looked to her drink, now almost halfway done, and then to her remaining friend—the one that was currently not rubbing her hand up the thigh of the dude in the Carhartt cap.

"Mitz. You ready to go?"

Mitzi Summerdale, who had been called Mitz by all of her friends since middle school looked to her as if she were crazy.

"Um, no. It's just barely past midnight. Last call isn't for another hour." She frowned in a playful way and then shook her head. "Worried about a hangover in church tomorrow?"

Tara bristled. "No. Jesus loves me the way I am, thanks."

Mitzi laughed and downed the last of her martini. She looked over to their other friend, Cassandra, and rolled her eyes.

"Gross, right?" Tara said.

52

"Yeah. I love her, but Cassandra is about as easy as a Highlights crossword. Now...tell you what. You take a shot with me and split cab fare, and we can go. I think Cassandra is covered for a ride tonight."

Both women snickered at this as a hand reached out and took their empty glasses. When Tara looked at the bartender, she realized he was cute. Not her type, but cute.

"You need another?" he asked.

Mitzi answered for them. "No. But we do need two shots."

"Of what?"

Mitzi smiled at him in a flirty way. Apparently, she thought he was cute, too. "Surprise us. Something strong. This is going to be the closer for the night."

"Challenge accepted." With that, the bartender eyed both of them flirtatiously and set about making their drinks.

Staring at him, Mitzi said, "Maybe we could get HIM to give us a ride home."

Tara was about to respond with a crude remark but her phone buzzed on the table beside her. She checked the caller ID and saw that it was her mother. And she was *calling*, not texting.

"Shit."

"Mommy calling?" Mitzi joked.

"Cram it." She took the phone and slid out of her seat. "Don't you dare do that shot without me."

Mitzi gave a salute, an aye-aye sort of gesture, as Tara walked out of the bar and out onto the street. The last thing she wanted was her mother to hear the telltale murmur of a bar in the background.

Making sure to keep her irritation under control, Tara answered the call.

"Hey, Mom. What's up?"

"You're out, aren't you?"

"Yes. With Cassandra and Mitzi."

"Ah, Lord. Are you drunk?"

"No. We had a few drinks, but I'm fine."

"It's midnight. You should be home."

Tara wasn't sure where this was coming from. Her mother had always been strict but as of late, she'd resorted to this stage of acting as if Tara was a fifteen-year-old again. She got particularly antsy if she knew Tara was going out on a Saturday. Tara assumed this was because her mother was afraid people in church might somehow find out that her previously little Tara enjoyed drinking and having fun at all hours of the night.

"I know. We're about get a cab."

She waited for her mother's rebuttal, but nothing came. Instead, all she got was a disappointed-sounding closing line. "I'll pick you up for the 8:30 service. See you then."

And then there was a dead line in Tara's ear.

"Love you, too, Mom," Tara said to the silent phone.

She pocketed it and started for the door to the bar again. She was JUST pissed enough to take another three shots with Mitzi rather than the one that was already waiting.

Yet, as she reached out for the door, she heard something off to her left. It was faint and barely there, but she heard it.

Weeping. Soft and muffled.

She walked to the edge of the bar and looked down the small alleyway that ran between the bar and the trendy coffee shop. Being after midnight, the café was, of course, closed.

The alley was surprisingly clean. A few plastic garbage containers sat perched along the buildings and further back, she could see the employee exit hidden in the shadows.

As she took it all in, she heard the weeping sound again. It was louder now, a bit more prominent.

"Hello?" she called out.

The crying noise stopped for a moment. Somewhere in the distance, about a block or so down, she could hear people chattering and laughing about something. It sounded odd as she stared down the alley.

And that's when she saw the huddled shape on the ground.

She started moving forward before she realized what she was doing. She figured it might just be a homeless person, or maybe someone that had started drinking very early in the day and had passed out in the alley.

But they'd been crying. Maybe someone was hurt. Maybe someone had been stabbed or something.

She stepped closer to the shape on the ground. As she closed in, small alarm bells started to ring in her head. Something was wrong here. She was making a mistake. She was…

The whimpering continued. It was real, legitimate. Not a cry of pain but something else.

She came to the shape on the ground. It was definitely a person, wrapped in what looked like a filthy blanket of some kind, or maybe a large coat.

"Hello? Are you okay?"

She wondered what the hell she was thinking. She could hear her mother scolding her for being such a fool.

"Are you hurt?" she asked.

The crying stopped again and the shape under the blanket or coat or whatever it was shifted a bit.

"Are you okay?" she asked again.

"No," the shape said. "Please..."

A shiver crawled up Tara's spine. Something was wrong here. Suddenly, the alley didn't feel safe. She wanted to leave. She wanted to run. She wanted to be home and in her bed, last shot with Mitzi be damned.

What the hell was going on here? Was this some sort of a trap or something?

She stepped away slowly.

The shape beneath the cover moved so quickly that she was barely aware of what was happening.

A large hand wrapped around her wrist and pulled her down to the ground. She opened her mouth to scream but the filthy blanket or coat was shoved into her mouth. Somewhere distantly she felt a slight pinch just along her waist.

And after that, everything went completely dark.

CHAPTER TWELVE

Camille was willing to admit that she'd wanted to head out onto the busy French Quarter streets on a Saturday night to prove she could do it. While it was the French Quarter itself that she had a bad taste for, it was a pretty significant landmark for an area she had come to despise.

Still, the streets of the French Quarter seemed to push the woodlands she'd grown up in even further away. Here, her home in Upping could have been on the other side of the world. It was a nice thought but her heart knew better. Her heart knew just how close Upping was...and that in a very skewed and messed up sort of way, Camille still considered it home.

She did her best to put her childhood home, her father, and her wretched past out of her mind as she patrolled the streets. She had a killer to find, after all. She couldn't let her past get in the way of that.

So she continued forward, working her way through streets that were both familiar and alien at the same time. There was a downtown feel to everything, right down to the construction and decorations of the buildings but, as was the case with most of New Orleans, there was just a much larger feeling of grandness to it all. It was a subtle type of city, the excitement and glamor of it hidden most of the time.

It was a strange feeling to be in a place where so many people were separated from one another by nothing more than a few feet and yet feel so alone. Camille knew the feeling was only amplified by the fact that she'd conditioned herself to have negative feelings towards this city but knowing this did nothing to ease it.

Camille had been surprised that she had seen so little of the infamous drunken debauchery the area was known for as she'd made her way through that part of the city. Still, it seemed like the French Quarter had an underlying buzzing spirit, the sort of place that was going to have a good time with or without its usual stereotypical fuss.

She heard loud music and singing from some of the bars, and rowdy yelling from others. She did not go inside any of them, though. The killer had been abducting women, which meant he was likely lying in wait. She imagined he would stake out a woman, find out what bar or hangout she frequented, and wait there.

In other words, she did not expect to find a killer by going inside the bars. She figured she stood a better chance if she simply did her own stake-out, checking the shadows and alleyways around the bars and lounges.

She was drawing near a street corner she'd passed earlier when she saw her first sign of potential trouble.

On the other side of the street, a woman had just come out of a bar, swaying a bit and laughing. She was giggling into her phone, speaking in a hushed yet silly manner to someone. As she left the bar and started walking to the right, a man that had been sitting on the curb sat up quickly. He glanced around for a moment and then, after a bit of thought, started following the woman.

It was more than enough to interest Camille. She waited for the man to get just out of her line of sight and then followed him. She crossed the street and then followed a good distance behind him on the sidewalk. Ahead of them, the woman had gotten off of her phone and was ambling by herself in the dark.

Camille followed behind the man. He walked with his head down and his hands in his pockets. Camille was certain he had nothing good in mind.

He was not much taller than the woman, and was thin and wiry, like a coiled spring. Every now and then, he would make a point to look up, keeping tabs on the woman.

Then, suddenly, he stopped. When he did, he bent over and acted as if he were tying his shoe. Not wanting to be caught or found out, Camille kept walking. She passed by him and spotted the unsuspecting woman just ahead. She had also stopped. She was texting something on her phone, near a group of five people.

Camille passed a few feet ahead of the man, looking into a bar window and pretending to watch what was going on inside. Out of the corner of her eye, she saw the woman start moving again.

Unsurprisingly, the man she'd been following also stood upright again and followed.

About a minute later, the woman turned left. She walked into a public parking lot which was only partially filled. It was well-lit but there was no one in it.

Ahead of Camille, the man started to move quickly toward the woman. Camille also started to walk faster as the man closed the distance between him and the woman.

57

Camille knew she could not go for her gun. not yet. She didn't know for sure this was her guy. It could just be some random creep. And she didn't want to pull her gun unless absolutely necessary.

As Camille got closer to the man, he was suddenly right next to the woman. He did not reach out and try to grab her. Instead, he spoke. As he did, Camille ducked down behind a truck. She had to catch this creep in the act, had to know without a doubt if it was the killer or not.

"You scream, I'll kill you."

Camille watched from the corner of the truck. The man and the woman were no more than ten feet away.

"Look, just leave me alone okay?" she asked. "I really don't want to get into it all with cops, but I will. So just beat it. Creep."

"I just want one thing from you. Give it to me, and you can get home to your nice, warm bed."

Camille watched the man's hands, making sure he did not go for a weapon. He had nothing to attack her with, just his bare hands, but attacking was apparently not his agenda.

His hands moved to the waist of his pants.

"Just one thing, sweetheart," he said. "Just me and you and no one else needs to know."

Camille heard the man's zipper coming down.

"Fuck off," the woman said.

"Aww, you want to be like that?" the man chuckled.

That was enough for Camille. With her fists clenched, she pivoted away from the truck and stepped into view.

"Hold it right there," she said.

The man wheeled around, his hands still at his zipper. "And who the hell are you? You want some, too?"

"Not quite. I'm with the FBI. Zip your pants and step away from the woman."

She stepped closer to the man. He had a faint glaze in his eyes. He'd apparently been drinking.

"No way you're a cop, sweet thing. Show me your badge. Or better yet, show me your tits."

"My badge or my...what?"

He grinned at her, clearly a little drunk and not thinking clearly.

"Or your t—"

Camille punched him hard in the chin and slammed his face into a nearby car.

She brought her knee up and then punched him in the gut. Once, twice, three times.

"You should have just let me arrest you, asshole."

The man moaned from the ground.

"You okay?" Camille asked the woman.

"Y-Yeah. Thank you. Thank you so much."

Camille only nodded, looking down to the man on the ground. "Sure. Now get home."

The woman nodded and raced to a car three spots over, fumbling with the keys to get inside.

Camille bent over the man she'd deeply taken down. When she started to search his pockets, he tried to slap her away. He received a hard forearm shot to the face for his efforts.

As he lolled his head back and forth, she checked his pants pockets but found only a wallet. No syringes, no vials of liquid.

She wasn't surprised, really. A guy that was as bold and blatant as to take his pants down on an unsuspecting woman in a parking lot was NOT the sort of man she was looking for. No, her killer would have been more subtle and probably not half-drunk.

"I'm going to arrest you," she said as she stood up.

"Go to hell."

"Good come back. Now, before I cuff you, I need you to zip your pants back up."

"Why don't you zip 'em for me?"

"Maybe I kick you in the balls and then *make* you do it?"

The man reached for his zipper but that was the last thing Camille saw of him. Just as she reached for her cuffs, she heard two female voices calling out into the night.

"Tara? Hey, where the hell did you go?"

Camille turned toward the voices and saw two younger women approaching the parking lot. They looked irritated and a little scared. One of them saw the man on the ground and then Camille standing over him.

"Something wrong, girls?" Camille asked.

One of them, the shorter of the two, stepped forward. She looked back down to the still-moaning man and then back to Camille.

"You a cop or something?"

"FBI agent. Why? What's wrong?"

The two girls looked at one another and Camille noticed that the taller one looked like she might be on the verge of crying.

59

"It's our friend, Tara. She was with us at a bar half an hour ago but now...well, now we can't find her."

CHAPTER THIRTEEN

He tossed the blanket into the same trashcan he'd pulled it out of and looked back down to the woman. She'd passed out within seconds of the injection and her eyes were closed. She'd dropped her phone in the midst of the commotion. It was there, on the ground. He slammed his foot down hard on it. He had to do it three times for any effect because the damned things were built like tanks these days.

With the phone in a jumbled mess of wires and metal, he scooped it up and tossed it into the trashcan. He shifted things around, placing the blanket over it so the phone would remain hidden. He then went back to the girl and placed his own phone in her pocket. It was a paranoid safety measure but better to play it safe.

Just in case.

He then scooped the girl up. With her eyes closed, she could have easily been sleeping. She looked peaceful. Serene.

They all did at this point in the ritual.

He eyed the alleyway behind him and found it clear. There were a few late-night stragglers on the other side of the street, but they were far too focused on one another. He then looked straight ahead, toward the back lot where he'd parked his car.

There was only darkness ahead. He walked deeper into the shadows, knowing no one would see him now from the other end of the alley.

He'd parked his car as close to the alley as possible, behind a second-rate Chinese restaurant. Barring some colossal screw-up, he was home free already.

Ah, but he couldn't get too cocky. He had to make sure every step was meticulous and perfect.

He stepped further into the darkness of the alley. He felt safe there, especially with the comatose girl in his arms.

He couldn't help but smile. Was it really going to be this easy?

Maybe not. As he neared the back lot, something seemed wrong.

Something was about to happen. Someone...someone was nearby.

He reached the back lot, immediately feeling safer. The darkness behind him was now joined by darkness ahead of him. He took a few more steps and then reached the back of the restaurant. He shifted the woman slightly in his arms, changing his grip on her.

His car was right there, just twenty feet away. He'd intentionally parked in a relatively well-lit area so his car would not seem suspicious.

He walked a bit faster toward it. And that's when he heard the footsteps. There were two of them, and they grew louder as they approached.

He looked to the edge of the lot and saw two figures.

Cops. Good Lord, that's what cockiness got him, he supposed.

They both stopped as they spotted him. He knew what it looked like. A man carrying an unconscious girl out of a back alley, toward his car.

This had the potential to go very bad.

One of the cops placed his hand on the butt of his holstered pistol.

"Woah there," one of the cops said. "What the hell is this?"

The man did his best to sound afraid. He wasn't, not really. He was protected. But the cops didn't know that. They had no way of knowing what he was a part of.

"Yeah, Jesus," he said. "I know what this looks like."

"Do you now?" one of the cops said. He was the shorter of the two, but with an impressive build. The other was an overweight, middle-aged African American man.

"This is my daughter. She called me, slurring her speech about half an hour ago. She thought someone had put something in her drink. She asked me to come get her. To take her to her apartment."

"Sure, sir," the fat one said. "You expect us to believe that?"

"I don't...wait. Look, hold on. Her phone. Her phone is probably in her pocket. There's probably pictures of us on it."

The cops exchanged a glance and then the short one came closer.

They were standing at the back of his car now. The short one carefully reached into the girl's front pocket and took the cell phone out.

The phone was set to Face ID unlock, so the cop had to show it to him. "Fine," he said. "If it's your daughter, what's the passcode?"

"I'm not sure. Probably her mother's birthday. Try one, zero, two, two."

The cop punched the code in and the phone unlocked. He looked uneasily to his partner and showed it to him. The photo on the home screen showed two girls, both smiling—the girl in his arms was in the center. Or, rather, a girl that looked very much like her. It was hard to tell from the way her hair was laying partially over her face.

The cop looked from the picture and then to the face of the girl he held.

This was the only time he panicked. They didn't look like twins, but there were lots of resemblances. As if to appease his curiosity, the smaller cop opened up the photos app and scanned around.

Victory, he thought. Because of course there were pictures of that same girl posing with him. The girl in those pictures was his daughter. And the girl in his arms looked very much like her.

The short cops frowned and placed the phone on the back of his car.

"Where does she live?" the cop asked.

"Bleaker Ave."

"She still live with you?"

"No. Moved out as soon as she turned eighteen. I'm over on Everton."

The cops nodded in unison. "Sorry about that, sir," the short one said. "But you have to understand how this looks."

"Oh, of course. And I appreciate you men doing your job."

"You need anything?" the fat one asked.

"Nope. We're good. I think maybe we'll have a talk tomorrow. She...well, she does this a little too often."

The fat cop had already turned away from him, headed off to find other crimes.

The short one stepped to the car and actually opened the passenger side door for him so he could get the girl inside. He had to bite back a laugh at this.

"Good luck with it all," the cop said.

"Thanks."

He placed the girl into the passenger seat and walked over to the driver's side as the cops headed back across the lot.

He did not wait until they were gone to move. That would have seemed suspicious. He backed out and even waved at them as he passed.

He didn't realize how tense he was until he was out on the street with the back parking lot behind the Chinese place a mile or so behind him.

That had been too close. There was way too much attention on the area now. Soon, the two women he'd already taken would be all over the news. He was pretty sure the FBI was already in town.

63

He was going to have to move his base soon.
After this girl, he'd have to find somewhere else to hunt.

CHAPTER FOURTEEN

Palmer was muttering under his breath as he got behind the wheel of his car. It was 1:05 in the morning and Camille Grace expected him to just come running when she called. She'd called ten minutes ago from some parking lot out in the French Quarter. He'd been so abruptly woken up that he didn't even think to ask her what the hell she'd been doing there when she was supposed to be at a hotel.

He let out a yawn as he pulled away from the curb in front of his apartment building. Excitement stirred in his stomach. Certainly she wouldn't have called unless it was important. He wouldn't know, though; she'd not given any details over the phone.

Palmer cranked up the volume on the car stereo. Bluetooth had instantly connected to his phone, and the ear-shattering sounds of Rammstein filled the car. It was more than enough to bring him fully awake as he drove through the night toward the alleyway where Camille had asked him to meet her.

The drive took about twenty minutes thanks to the thin very-early morning traffic. When he pulled his car into the parking lot, he saw a police car that had pulled slightly off to the side—not blocking the lot from traffic, but making it known that some shit was going down.

The passenger side door to the cruiser was open, with a young-looking woman occupying the seat. A cop sat behind the wheel and nearly got out to stop Palmer as he parked his car. Palmer got out, showed his badge, and the cop relaxed.

Palmer took a quick look around, scanning for Camille. The lot was poorly lit, and he had to squint to see. What had caused her to come out here, anyway? Has she been hiding leads? Or was she just *that* committed to her job?

He finally spotted her several spaces down. She was standing in front of a car, with another woman sitting on the hood. The woman was smoking a cigarette and speaking softly to Camille. He walked over to join them and instantly noticed the look of intensity in Camille's eyes.

"What's going on?" he asked.

"Agent Palmer, this is Mitzi Summerdale. I'll let her tell you what's happened."

The girl, quite pretty but clearly filled with worry, took one final drag off of her smoke before flicking it across the lot. It came down several feet away in a little plume of sparks.

"We were out drinking," she said. "Me, Tara, and Cassandra. Tara got a call from her mom and headed out of the bar to take it. And then...she just sort of disappeared."

"You mean she never came back into the bar?"

"That's right. And so I figured she decided to go home. That maybe her mom had guilted her into it, you know? But we all took an Uber out tonight, knowing we'd probably be in no shape to drive. And before she stepped out to take the call, we'd joked about sharing a ride, splitting the fare."

"Any chance she would have just left in a hurry?"

"Not without telling me," Mitzi said. "She's not the type. She would have at least texted me to let me know she had to bounce."

"Any chance her mother may have come by and taken her?"

"Doubtful. That woman thinks the French Quarter is the Seventh Ring of Hell. She's pretty religious."

"Have you tried calling her?" Palmer asked.

"Yeah. It rings like once and then starts clicking. Not even picking up voice mail."

He looked to Camille thoughtfully. "That means it's not turned off."

"I thought the same thing," Camille said. She then looked to Mitzi and said, "Do you guys do the whole Friends and Family thing where you can see where one another is by tracking their phone?"

"No, we...wait, yes! We turned it on when we went to Universal Studios a few weeks ago!"

Mitzi flocked her phone and opened up the feature. She seemed excited, hoping this would answer their questions.

"This makes no sense. It says she's back at the bar."

Camille looked at it and shook her head. "No. It's just reading her last known location."

"Usually that means the phone is off," Palmer said. "But if it's ringing and then giving that click..."

"It's likely been tossed," Camille finished.

"Mitzi, do you have a picture of Tara?"

"Yeah, sure." She opened her photo apps, scrolled for a moment, and then pulled one up. She showed it to the agents. Palmer saw a girl in her early twenties, blonde hair and beautiful almond-shaped eyes.

"Here. Let me text that to myself."

Mitzi handed over her phone and Palmer worked quickly to send the picture to his phone. "Okay, Mitzi. We're going to take you over to the cop over there. I assume that's your other friend with him?"

"Yeah, that's Cassandra."

"He'll watch after you, maybe ask a few more questions. But really, I think the two of you can go home. We'll be looking for Tara. And we'll start at the bar and work our way out."

Mitzi nodded and hopped off the hood of the car. She followed the agents to the cop car and when they parted, Mitzi looked defeated. It appeared as if she was expecting bad news at any moment.

When they were standing by Palmer's car, Camille lowered her voice, looking back to the cop car.

"You saw the last known location on the map. It's right down the street. Maybe four blocks, right?"

"Right. I know where the bar is."

"If the phone is still on but disposed of or broken, that's not a good sign," she said

"Yeah, I know. Maybe we walk. Check alleys, parking lots, check for any sketchy folks."

"Yeah, I had a run-in with that sort earlier."

"Really?" he asked. "Are you okay?"

"Oh, yeah, I'm fine. The other guy, though..."

She trailed off here, as if she didn't really want to have to explain the rest of it.

"What guy?" Palmer asked.

"I'll tell you later. For now, let's just focus on this case."

"Okay," he said skeptically. "Well, I did notice that the picture we saw of Tara...there's a pretty good resemblance to Sara and Victoria."

"You think he has a specific type?"

"Maybe," Palmer said. "So far it seems that they all have blonde hair, with larger eyes."

"I suppose that could help from here on out."

They went quiet after that, and Palmer could sense that they were thinking the same thing: if a woman *had* been abducted nearby, the abductor only had about an hour on them. Maybe an hour and a half at most.

They walked the dark streets, weaving through some of the remaining revelers. Most of the bars had already called last call, so there wasn't much for the crowds to do. After covering the four blocks quickly, they came to the bar Mitzi, Tara, and Cassandra had visited.

"We know Sara Berringer was in this area, somewhere around bars, just before she was taken," Camille said. "Victoria Hudson is a question mark, but based on this current moment, I'm willing to put money on her having frequented a bar, too. So the killer is lurking, watching..."

She looked around, her eyes going to the first obvious location. There was an alleyway between the bar and the neighboring building, a coffee shop. Palmer had noticed it, too, but thought it might be a little brazen for a killer to lurk around there, so close to what was surely a packed bar when drinks were still being served.

Without discussing it, Camille started down the alley. Palmer followed, taking a moment to appreciate the way Camille studied the scene. She eyed everything: the walls of each building along the alley, the ground, even the sky. He wondered if she was looking for clouds, maybe trying to track where the moon would have been positioned two hours ago if there had indeed been a killer here.

"You really think a killer would snatch a woman up in a place like this?" he asked. "Seems a little close to a heavily populated area."

"It's the French Quarter. Every area is heavily populated. It's a dark alley and no one with partying in mind is going to pay much attention to it."

It was a very good point, so he followed her in. She was right. It was very dark: he hadn't realized just HOW dark until he took a few steps into the alley.

He looked at the ground, which was covered in shadows. A few garbage cans, beer bottles, two random trash bags sitting out on their own.

Camille was looking closely at the ground—a painstaking task, given that neither of them had come with a flashlight. Camille used the flashlight mode on her phone and it did a moderate job at best.

"What are you looking for?" he asked.

"Something that could have kept a person quiet. Mitzi said Tara left the bar when she got a call from her mother. I wonder if she may have been just distracted enough by the intrusion on her night to not notice someone about to pounce on her. And if it was our killer, he'd want to keep her quiet, right? There have been no prints on the bodies so far, so he's being careful..."

She stopped here, looking at the garbage can that sat about a quarter of the way down the alley. She cautiously opened the lid and peered inside.

"Something like this," she said.

Palmer joined her at the trash can. He peered inside and saw an old ratty canvass-style blanket.

He wasn't at all surprised when Camille once again pulled out her latex gloves and slapped them on. She then lifted the blanket out and set it on the ground.

"It would keep his prints off her body and could also be used to muffle her screams," she said.

Palmer wasn't quite ready to say she was making a stretch here, desperate to find something. But he felt it. For a killer to take a victim here, so close to the bar...it didn't feel right.

Almost idly, he stepped to the trashcan and looked inside.

"I'll be damned," he said.

"What is it?"

She stood up and looked inside, too. For a second or two they both simply looked down at the mostly-ruined shape of an iPhone. The bottom portion was barely held together, but the top was mostly ruined. The screen had been splintered into countless pieces, a few sections showing the inner workings of the phone behind it.

"How much do you want to bet that's Tara's?" Camille asked.

Still looking to the ruined phone, Palmer said: "This is New Orleans, not Vegas. And I don't like the odds."

***

With the assistance of the same policeman that had seen to it that Mitzi and Cassandra found a safe ride home, Camille was able to bag up the wrecked iPhone. And now that they had suspicion of not only a missing woman but a suspected victim of their killer, more cops had arrived on the scene quickly to help.

Camille was thoroughly investigating the alleyway with a flashlight she'd borrowed from one of the cops when Palmer came out of the bar. The bar was closed now, as it was just after two in the morning, but Camille and Palmer, as well as few other cops, had been going in and out.

Palmer gave her a shrug as he came over to where she was currently tracing the ground with the flashlight. "The bartender says he remembers her, but nothing in particular about her. He says the only guy that was near Mitzi and her friends was an innocent enough guy that was pretty close to getting lucky with Cassandra."

"No unreal or shady characters all night?"

"Not according to him."

Camille shook her head, looking down the rest of the alley. "We need to talk to her mother. We need to see if any of the businesses around here have security cameras that would have caught anything."

"I already asked the bartender about that. He says they have three exterior angles on their security feeds. One of them may have caught the guy coming into the alley, but it wouldn't catch anything in the alley."

"That may have to be good enough for now." She was irritated and getting slightly anxious. The case was quickly getting away from her. It felt bigger now, more unpredictable.

Also, this much police presence around the area where he was striking was probably going to result in the killer taking up his stakes and moving elsewhere.

In other words, if they didn't solve this case soon, the killer stood a good chance of getting away.

"Hey...Grace. You okay?"

She looked to Palmer and nodded, though she was not okay. Not really.

But he didn't need to know that.

"I'm fine."

"You sure? You seem shaken. I know I don't know you all that well, but still..."

"I'm fine." She repeated more firmly, though now it was more for herself than for him. "I just need to focus. You know?"

What she didn't want to tell him was the damned city itself seemed to be interfering with her mind. Her thoughts were starting to feel hazy and abstract. Maybe she was just tired.

"Hey, agents?"

They both turned and saw a pair of policemen walking toward them. One was rather short and the other, a black man, was overweight and looked nervous about something.

"Yeah?" Camille asked.

"Hey," the short one said. "We're Officers Lawrence and Kohl. We stopped by to check to see if there was anything we could do about this situation and...well, we heard something that..."

"What is it?" Camille asked, already irritated with the man's hesitancy.

"We stopped a man that was carrying a woman to his car earlier. Right at the other end of this alley."

"Where is he?" Palmer asked.

"We let him go."

"What?" Camille barked. "Are you *kidding* me?"

"Hey, calm down," the fat one said. "His story checked out. He said it was his daughter, that she'd had too much to drink. He let us take her phone. He knew the code and everything. There were pictures of him and the girl on the phone."

"You're certain of this?" Camille asked.

"Yeah, we saw the pictures with our own eyes."

"But you're *sure* it was the same girl he was carrying?"

"Well, I mean she was passed out," the short one said. "It looked just like her...but her eyes were closed and her hair was in her face and—"

"When?" she said, growing furious with the pair.

"Two hours ago, give or take."

"For God's sake," Palmer muttered.

"Show us where," Camille said. "But first get on the horn to your sheriff. Tell him we need a manhunt out in the woods to the west of here. If he needs to talk to me, tell him to wait a second because I'm canvassing an area where you two allowed a man to leave with an unconscious woman."

Both men looked as if they'd been slapped.

"Where?" she asked again, nearly screaming it this time.

"I'll show you," the short one said, hurrying out in front of her.

As Camille and Palmer followed him, the overweight cop made the call to the station. Camille heard him give the order, letting everyone on the other end know that there was a suspected third victim and a manhunt was needed out in the woods.

Out in the woods where Camille was already very afraid they'd find another dead woman.

CHAPTER FIFTEEN

Once again, Camille was sitting in the passenger seat while Palmer drove. It was his car now rather than the bureau-issued sedan that they'd used earlier in the day. The lights and well-defined streets of New Orleans began to sink away to their left as Palmer drove them out to the more rural outskirts for the second time that day.

"I thought you were going to find a hotel," Palmer said. He did not sound confused or disappointed. He sounded a little angry, actually.

"I figured that time might be better spent looking for the killer."

"On your own?"

"I didn't expect you to pull an all-nighter with me."

"If you'd just suggested it, I might have come along."

"It's not a big deal. I just figured maybe it was worth walking around the killer's stomping grounds. Trying to think like him. To get into his mindset."

"And did it work?"

She thought of the sexual assault she'd stopped, particularly how the man's head had felt when she'd bounced it from a car. "In a roundabout way."

"I want to solve this case as badly as you," he said. "But I'd really like to be on the same page, if possible. No secret agendas or missions, please."

"Fair enough. I'm sorry I went rogue. When I'm on the road for a case, I don't tend to sleep well. And being this close to...to my history isn't helping."

"Some bad stories from your childhood?"

"Yeah."

"Want to share?"

"No."

"What about the Sir Richard Case? Want to tell me how you finally snagged him?"

She thought about it but they were interrupted by a call to Palmer's phone. She was glad he was the point of contact on this case. There was nothing Camille hated more than a constantly ringing phone.

He answered it and she listened in as he placed it on speaker.

72

"Hey, Agent Palmer, this is Officer Reeves. We've got a unit headed over to the mother's house right now. And there are currently three units heading for three different points along the stretch of woods you indicated."

"Good. Thanks. Keep us posted. We're headed there ourselves."

Short and to the point, he ended the call. He then looked over and carried on as if they'd never been interrupted.

"They say you can get into the mind of a killer. Is that right?"

"Sort of."

"Do you have a profile for our guy yet?"

"I'm getting there."

"Want to share?"

She sighed and did her best to explain the thoughts and fragmented theories in her head.

"There's something about this that feels personal."

"Personal?"

"Yeah. Personal. There's a reason he's doing this. A reason he's choosing these victims."

"You mentioned voodoo earlier. You still thinking along those lines?"

"Yes. Voodoo is just like any religion. It can feel intimate and personal. And if it IS at the core of this, it might help us figure out why he's choosing the women that he's choosing."

"Something like a ritual? Something symbolic?"

"Maybe. Actually, if there's voodoo involved, it's very likely."

"So you're saying that he's choosing them because of some personal reason, potentially connected to voodoo?"

"I'm not saying that exactly. I'm saying that each of them has something in common. Something they have in common with each other. Consider Victoria and Sara. They looked alike, don't you think?"

"Yeah, maybe a bit. Both young, both attractive but not overly so. Blonde hair, almond-shaped brown eyes."

"Tara, in her pictures. She's pretty, too." She thought this over, trying to clearly recall images of Sara and Victoria in her head. Did they all look slightly alike? She'd need to see pictures side-by-side to be sure. But she did recall Palmer saying something along those lines after speaking with Tara's friends and texting himself the picture of Tara.

"Well, we can't just start sending out cops to protect pretty girls," Palmer said.

Camille knew he meant it as tension-breaking remark, but it fell flat. It was just as well, because Palmer was currently turning off of a featureless two-lane road and onto a thin, dirt track. They drove about fifty yards down it before they were stopped by a chain across the road.

"Where are we?"

"The D'Amour property. A rich family. This little road serves as a conduit for a lot of other roads that venture out into the woods. Little cut-overs and fields. For the D'Amours, it just goes out to a big fishing pond. It's not all connected, but I'd consider this the center of this stretch of woodland. And these woods apparently mean something to the killer, right?"

"Yeah, I think that's safe to say."

Together, they hiked out into the forest. Now equipped with flashlights, their beams bobbed and hovered over the ground like confused ghosts.

"You really think he would have put her out here already?" Palmer asked.

"I think so. If he's so blatant as to take a girl from an alley by a busy bar, I assume he's working quickly."

The nighttime insects buzzed and flitted around them. Tree frogs groaned and whip-poor-wills sang.

Off to the left, further off in the trees, she saw other shafts of light. "Other cops?" she asked.

"Yeah. They would have come in on the backside of the D'Amour property."

Camille nodded as they made their way deeper into the trees. "You know these woods well? Would you happen to know where the clearings and fields are?"

"Sorry...no."

They stayed close together, walking in the darkness around trees. Memories of her childhood came back, memories of gigging for frogs with her father—back before so much bad stuff had happened. Before her father had become something else. Back before...

Nope, she thought. Not now. Not out here.

But if not here, then when? Where? She knew she was going to have face these ghosts before she headed back to Birmingham.

A faint sound tore through these thoughts. Faraway, but noticeable. She thought it might be the other cops about two hundred yards out to the left, but no...it had come from just ahead, slightly to the right.

She stopped and turned around, redirecting the flashlight. Palmer stopped alongside her and did the same.

A weighty silence filled the forest.

"You hear that?" she asked.

"Yeah. Maybe a footstep. Something crunchy, on the ground."

They both listened closely. It came again, soft and cautious. Something moving quietly along the forest floor. If it *was* a footstep, it was someone that was trying to move slowly, going unseen.

After a few more steps, it came again, from the same direction. She looked to Palmer and gave him a hand sign, pointing to herself, and then to the right at a hard angle. He nodded and did the same, pointing ahead.

They broke apart and tried chasing the source of the noise down. It wasn't a cop and it wasn't some woodland creature as far as she could tell.

It was a single, deliberate step, and whoever it was, they were trying to be quiet.

She poked her head around a tree and found nothing but more trees on the other side. Palmer was off to her right, doing the same. She started moving forward.

And then there it was again, further away this time. All she could hear was the crunching of leaves and twigs as it moved away from her.

The stealthy footsteps were moving away and she didn't have time to wait. If it was the killer, he could hide away easily in the trees and shadows of night. There was no time to waste.

She ran through the forest, charging forward, breaking through brush, and cursing under breath, hoping she wasn't making too much noise.

She heard Palmer behind her and to the left. He was calling her name in a raised whisper.

But she charged ahead, waving aside low-hanging branches. She was so sure she might be on the heels of the killer that she switched the flashlight to her left hand and pulled out her Glock.

But it was at that very same moment that she found herself in a thin space that looked slightly different than the rest of the tree-lined forest to all sides. She was standing on a patch of moss, looking at a nearly rectangular patch of forest that was around ten feet long by five feet wide.

There was a ragged old stump in the center, likely a relic of some long ago rot.

A body was lying on it. A female body, naked. The stump was not very large, so the body was arched at the back, the abdomen tilted up. The woman's head was arched back and down, her hair pooling on the green moss.

Camille knew what she was seeing, but she trained the flashlight on it anyway.

It was Tara. She recognized the face from the picture on Mitzi Summerdale's phone. Camille felt something deflate inside of her— hope, she supposed. She truly thought they'd get to this girl before the killer acted. And now here she was, another dead young woman. And while Camille knew it was not solely her fault, she couldn't help but wonder if Tara might still be alive if they'd been just a bit faster.

Standing frozen in place, she called softly out into the night.

"Palmer! She's here."

***

In less than five minutes, Palmer and three cops had joined Camille in the clearing. Five flashlight beams played over the nude body of the girl Camille only knew as Tara. She supposed Palmer may have gotten a last name, but she hadn't heard it yet.

Camille was shining her flashlight on Tara's hip, on the left side. Under the blaze of the flashlight, the injection site was plain to see. The fact that it had happened very recently helped, too.

The pinpricks in the valley between her breasts were there, too, just like Sara and Victoria.

"The son of a bitch couldn't have gotten far," Palmer said. "He had to carry the body out here, do whatever weird shit he had in mind, and then escape. So either he knows these woods like he's Daniel Boone, or we've missing something obvious. I'm open to theories on this one."

"I'll go look," Camille said, turning and already taking one huge stride back out into the darkness.

"Well, hold on now" one of the cops said. By his badge and nameplate on his left breast, Camille thought he was a deputy. "We've got road blocks set up five miles away from here in every direction. And there are at least two more units coming to help us check the forest floor."

Camille knew it was all that could be done for now. And even with that, searching the forest floor for anything of note was going to be a

76

fool's errand until the sun was out. The same was true of searching for the killer himself if he did know these woods well.

"An hour and a half, if that," Camille said. "That's how much of a lead this guy has on us."

It was infuriating to know that the killer had been in this very spot recently. It had her turning her flashlight to the ground, as if willing a clue to pop up—a loose hair, a fragment of clothing, *anything.*

But then she thought of what she'd told Palmer in the car. There was the strong probability that these three young women might have something in common. Yes, there was already their looks and their age. But what if there was something else?

"Hey, Palmer?"

He was clearly shaken. His face looked like a ghoul for a moment as he came over. "Yeah?"

"Mitzi said Tara had received a call from her mother, right?"

"Yeah."

"A call from her mother, just after midnight. On a Saturday. It might make sense if Tara was fifteen or sixteen and living at home. But this is a grown woman. Why would her mother call so late on a Saturday night?"

Palmer considered it for a moment. He looked to the body and then to the moss at their feet. He sighed deeply and shrugged. "No clue," he answered. "But maybe we should find out."

CHAPTER SIXTEEN

Whatever vestiges of weariness had lingered from having been woken up in the middle of the night were long gone from Palmer when he pulled his car into the driveway of Janet Maxwell's residence. According to the cops that had to explain to Janet that her daughter, Tara Maxwell, appeared to be missing, the woman was in hysterics.

Palmer hated to think of what it was going to be like when he and Camille told the woman that her daughter was dead. That her daughter was the third victim of a killer that was proving to be extremely elusive.

As it turned out, Janet Maxwell lived just fifteen minutes south of where her daughter's body had been discovered When he pulled his car into her driveway, a chill rode up his spine as he realized that during the day, Janet Maxwell would be able to see the woods where her daughter had died from her back porch.

Palmer walked very close to Camille as they made their way up the sidewalk. Janet was already at the door, still accompanied by one of the officers that had originally come by.

"How many times have you done this?" Palmer asked.

"You mean tell a parent that their kid has died?"

"Yeah."

"A few. Never when it was this fresh, though."

"I have. Once. I was really hoping to never have to do it again."

They made their way to the porch steps. Janet Maxwell looked out to them through her screen door. She looked to be in her fifties. And right away, she seemed to know. Palmer wondered if it was something in their faces or maybe just the way they were carrying themselves. Whatever the case, Janet Maxwell *knew* they had come with bad news.

She started to shake her head, her hands going to her face. As she sank to her knees, the cop opened the door for them. There was a grim look on his face, his mouth a tight, thin line.

"Don't you tell me," Janet said. Her blue eyes looked like wet crystals as she gazed up to them. "Don't you dare..."

"Mrs. Maxwell," Camille said.

78

And then the woman simply seemed to break. "She's gone? She's GONE? No...No, not my Tara! Don't you tell me that!"

"I'm afraid we have to," Palmer said, stepping forward and placing a hand on the woman's shoulder. "Mrs. Maxwell, we found her body in—"

"No!" She roared and slapped Palmer hard on the chest. She then collapsed into him. The cop that had been there already reached out to help steady her.

Janet roared against his chest. God, he'd never felt such hurt and anguish come out of someone like this.

"No! No my Tara! Not my baby!"

"I'm so sorry, ma'am," Palmer said.

"I want to see her. Now."

"We can't do that."

"I want to see her..."

"We can't do that," he repeated. "I'm so sorry." And he really was. God, he couldn't imagine the pain.

Janet stepped back, looking around as if she was expecting someone to jump out and tell her this was all a very bad prank. She took several deep, shuddering breaths as Palmer and Camille guided her back inside.

"Who? Who could have done this to my baby? Who would have done this to my baby? Why would they have done this to my baby?"

She kept repeating it over and over as they walked her back into the house. In the living room, she sank into the couch. Her entire body seemed to shudder.

"When can I go see her? I don't believe it. There's just no way she's d...d...dead..."

"We can't take you now," Camille said gently. "We are quite certain she is linked to two other young women that have been murdered recently. Right now, it's vital that we find anything we can that links h—"

"Murdered?" she wailed it and the end of it came out in an almost haunting sing-song fashion.

"Mrs. Maxwell, I know it's very hard," Palmer said. "But we need to ask some questions. We need to act while we can, right away."

"Yes...yes, okay, I can do that." She spoke through whimpers as her brain tried to process the weight of what she was hearing—the weight of what she'd have to live with every day after this.

79

Palmer knew they did not have much time. When it all caught up to Janet Maxwell, she would not be able to form a rational thought, much less answer any questions in a sensible fashion.

"Her friends...Cassandra and Mitzi. Do you know them?"

"Yes."

"Do you trust them?" Camille asked.

"I don't like the lives they live, but yes. They are good girls for the most part."

"Did Tara or her friends have any toxic ex-boyfriends that you know about?" Palmer asked.

Shit, he thought. He'd referred to Tara in the past tense. That was a no-no when questioning a relative of the recently deceased.

Apparently, Janet didn't notice. She shook her head and said, "Not that I know of."

"Ma'am," Camille said, "Is there anything at all you can tell us about Tara that may have angered someone? Anything at all, no matter how small it may seem?"

"She's a good girl. She loved her books and her writing. She's going to college for Library Sciences."

Palmer noted that she was referring to her daughter as if she was still alive.

"And she didn't have any enemies?" Palmer asked.

"No, of course not!" Janet's voice rose as if she was offended by the question. She then settled down as much as she could and, through a gut-wrenching whimper, she added: "She was a caring girl. She was strong-willed and she had a temper. She could be stubborn. I don't know what else you need me to say."

"Ma'am, why did you call her tonight?" Camille asked. Palmer was glad she had jumped so far forward in the questions. He sensed that this might be the last question they got out of Mrs. Maxwell.

"I knew she'd be out drinking. She's a woman now, so she can make her own decisions. But she goes to church with me every Sunday morning. I know she hates it, but she does it anyway. And now I...oh my God, I can't believe...she's really?"

"Church," Camille said. "She went with you? Is that why you called her? To make sure she was going with you in the morning?"

"Yes. She is...I mean...I," her thoughts were jumbling up. Palmer could not only hear it, but see it in her eyes. "She hated it. She doesn't believe in God like I do. So many questions and weird tendencies." She smirked sadly and shook her head. Tears went falling to the floor. "It's that Caribbean influence in her. That Creole nonsense."

"Creole?" Camille asked. "Tara is Creole?"

"Yes. Her father was. He left early in the marriage. With his dark, godless beliefs, I should have known."

Camille started for the front door so quickly that Palmer almost leaped up in surprise.

"I'm sorry, ma'am," Camille said. "Excuse me for one moment."

Palmer looked to the cop that remained by the front door apologetically, giving a look that communicated: Do you mind covering this for a moment?

The cop came walking over with a strained look.

Palmer excused himself and followed quickly after Camille, wondering what was going on. As he hurried down the stairs and followed her out to the car, he heard one more loud and piercing wail from Janet Maxwell before the screen door slammed shut behind him.

At the car, he found Camille leaning in, looking into the backseat.

"What's going on?" he asked.

"She's Creole, and...damn. Where are the case files?"

"At home. Don't you have the digital copies?"

She nodded and quickly pulled out her phone. But even as she started scrolling and clicking on her screen, it registered with Palmer. He thought he knew where she was going with this already and if it was right, it might make a huge difference in this case.

Camille started nodding after a few moments. "Yeah, here we go. Victoria Hudson...Creole by descent. And...," more scrolling, clicking, scrolling, "...the same for Sara Berringer. Creole."

"All three," Palmer said. "That can't be coincidental, can it?"

"Doubtful. Especially not if there's voodoo involved. You heard her in there," she said, hitching a thumb back to the house. "She specifically called out 'that Caribbean nonsense.'"

"How did this get missed?" Palmer asked, furious.

"Well, Tara is only half. And according to this, Victoria is only Creole by descent. It's not like they're living, breathing embodiments of the culture."

"So what does this tell us, exactly?"

"I don't know just yet," Camille said. "But being of Creole descent myself, I intend to find out."

81

CHAPTER SEVENTEEN

The manhunt turned up nothing and by the time the sun started peeking over the horizon, Camille knew it was going to be a bust. The State Police even had bloodhounds coming in and though she knew it was an effective method, she doubted it would do any good.

This was a very smart killer. He'd abducted a woman near a packed bar, swerved two policemen, and delivered her to the site out in the woods all within the space of two hours.

This told Camille two things. First, the killer had done this before. Second, he had planned everything out in meticulous detail.

Camille and Palmer, both weary-eyed but too amped up on adrenaline to truly be tired, sat in the back corner of the coffee shop located next to the bar where Tara Maxwell had last been seen alive. Both drinking black coffee, they looked over the case files. The coffee shop had just opened and the morning crowd had not yet truly arrived.

"Three women that all look similar," Palmer said, looking to the photos. Tara Maxwell's file was still very thin because her murder was so recent; it consisted of a single grainy picture printed off at the nearest precinct and a hastily written report.

"Would you say they look *remarkably* similar?" Camille asked.

"I don't know. I guess it depends on how they would be wearing their hair and makeup on any given day." He sighed and studied the pictures again. "So if the killer was going after them because they look alike *and* because of their Creole backgrounds, what does that tell us?"

"It tells us that he isn't a stereotypical serial killer. He doesn't just kill because they are women. He kills because they are Creole women; he has a very specific target in mind."

"And he is not like any serial killer I've ever seen," Palmer said. "No blood, no real violence to speak of. It's almost as if he's trying his best to preserve them."

"And that's what's tripping me up. So much stuff points to voodoo but something about the almost pristine presentation of the bodies doesn't quite line up."

"He keeps getting bolder, too. It makes me think he might almost be done. Or maybe he feels rushed now."

"I think we have to operate under the assumption that there are going to be more, and they may come at a quicker rate. But we also need to be prepared for the possibility that this guy may already be moving on somewhere else. There's a lot of pressure on him now. We were *really* closing in on him."

Palmer closed the file in front of him—Victoria Hudson's file—and rubbed at his head. "When we left Janet Maxwell's house, you said you were had some Creole in you. And you *just* said there are some elements about this case that don't align with voodoo. So let's go ahead and figure that out now. Do we proceed as if voodoo is at the center of this?"

"I think so," she said "Here's the thing. Voodoo is practiced among a lot of Creoles. So, it makes me think this might be a vengeance thing. Maybe the killer is attacking Creoles that aren't practicing voodoo. Tara Maxwell was going to church with her mother, after all. But then even *that* gets tricky because while no practitioners will openly admit it, voodoo is really just an adaptable set of beliefs. People can alter and change it around a bit to fit their given needs or situations. There's no sacred text like other religions, no real creeds of any kind to stick to."

"Any idea what the pin pricks on the chest could mean? Right between the breasts of young, attractive women. That's got to have significance, right?"

"Maybe something to do with the soul being taken? I don't know. I've heard of voodoo practitioners using pins to draw blood and act as a conduit for spirits to travel through. But there's no blood on these cases, so who knows?"

Palmer re-opened the file and looked at the marks in the pictures. "The same pattern, each time. No variation. Looks almost like small insect bites."

"I'm no expert on this stuff, but that could be the mark of Bondye."

"The mark of what?"

"Bondye. He's like the equivalent of God from Christian religions. It's a symbol of reverence to most but to some, it can also be used as a symbol of evil. It means that the person should have died, but didn't."

"But we're finding them dead."

"Yes, I know. It's making me think of neurotoxins. Secretions from the glands of a puffer fish."

"Grace...just...what?"

"There's legitimate reports out of Haiti of voodoo shamans forcing people to ingest deadly neurotoxins. Some think it's where the

83

Americanized version of zombies come from. Voodoo priests will make people ingest certain plaints or concoctions that will knock the person out...totally comatose, so out of it that an untrained doctor would think the person was dead. It was an experiment used for the purposes of the voodoo priests to make slaves."

"And this is for real?"

"Yes. A Harvard anthropologist did a study on it. Wrote a book on it and everything. *The Serpent and the Rainbow.*"

"And you think that's what's going on here?"

She shook her head but considered something. She'd just said something that had triggered an idea.

"What is it?" Palmer asked.

"An anthropologist...I need to speak to an anthropologist."

"Why?"

"Because in most universities, it's the anthropologists that have the best grasp and understanding on rituals in other cultures. And being that we're in Louisiana, I feel certain a local anthropologist could help is understand what's going on here if it *is* voodoo that we're dealing with."

"I've got a contact that can maybe get you a number from two local schools for that."

"The sooner the better." She drank down the rest of her coffee and looked at her watch. It was 6:05 and the day suddenly felt full of possibilities.

"But you know, maybe we should split up on this. No sense in both of us wandering around a university to speak to a professor."

"Okay. What will you be doing?"

"Maybe revisit some of the files from that first batch of killings. I think it might be of some use to also check the local criminal databases for locals with a history of violence toward Creole women."

"Sounds like a plan to me. Can you reach out to your contact for me?"

"Actually, now that I think about it..."

He pulled out his phone, opened up the browser and did a bit of typing. After about twenty seconds, he placed his phone on the table to show Camille.

"Go see this guy. Albert Penderhook. Professor of Anthropology at the University of Holy Cross. Right here in New Orleans. He helped a few local cops several months back when the remains of two skeletons were dragged from a pond."

84

Camille typed in his number and office information as she got to her feet. They made their way to the door and back out to Palmer's car.

"I need a car," Camille said.

"Hop in. I'll take you over to the nearest precinct and get you something."

"You work pretty close with the local PD from time to time, huh?"

"I do." And then, with an almost nervous tone, he added: "And it seems there's going to be a lot more of it if we want to find this guy."

It was a heavy statement, but one that sent them on their way, giving Camille an extra boost of energy and determination. She thought of the pin prick markings on the chest of the victims, the woods they'd been taken to, and the screams and wails of Janet Maxwell.

All three women were Creole...just like her.

Deep down, it did feel personal now.

And she was determined that one way or another, she was going to find this bastard.

CHAPTER EIGHTEEN

Palmer was beyond impressed with Camille Grace but at the same time, he was slightly relieved when they parted ways. It gave him time to ruminate on the morning, to better wrap his head around the case. He'd also done better work when he was by himself, even if it was something as simple as digging through old case files.

And that's exactly what he started doing when he got back to the precinct. He'd helped Camille get a precinct vehicle and then sat down at a desk located in a temporary office he'd used a handful of times in the past.

While drinking a cup of green tea, Palmer hunted through the precinct's digital records. He didn't think he'd have to call his field office to request special access to their database; chances were good that if there were records that would match what they were looking for or at least point them in the right direction, they'd be right here in the local PD files.

No one at the precinct knew him well. He was just the guy from the FBI's New Orleans field office that set up camp in their building every now and then. Therefore, he was left alone for the most part, able to work in peace and quiet.

By filtering the cases out by using "Creole" as a keyword, he was able to find what he was looking for rather easily. The tricky part was weeding through the thirty-six results to find ones that seemed to match their needs: cases that seemed to have a strong voodoo connection, and bodies that had little to no visible traces of assault.

After about an hour, he had it narrowed down to two cases. He read over the details, jotting down notes in his own notebook even as he printed the files out. He then read them while drinking another cup of tea.

The first file was quite short and told a simple yet tragic story.

The victim: a Luisa Beaulieu, a Creole woman. The cause of death: strangulation, followed by the slicing of her throat. She'd been killed and disposed of in the French Quarter last year, her body discovered in a garbage bin. The prints of the suspected killer had been found on her clothes...prints that had been linked to a similar attack a few weeks before but did not result in a death.

The suspect was a man name Clarence Obo, a local voodoo priest. He was also rumored to be a criminal mastermind, and he was wanted by the cops for questioning in a number of local murders. However, some of those murders were drug related.

He went to trial but was never convicted because of a lack of evidence and alibis that seemed rock solid.

Palmer wrote Clarence Obo's name down in a notebook on the desk.

The second case file was a bit more complex. He found himself studying almost as if it were a story rather than a case file.

The body of a female victim, Marie Cheri, was found in an abandoned building four or five days after she'd died. Her cause of death was strangulation but it was also evident that she had been mutilated. Her fingers, toes, and tongue were missing as was a section of skin from her shin. It looked as though they'd been removed with a knife.

The case was ruled a homicide and her boyfriend was charged. The boyfriend worked at a local voodoo shop. He admitted to having a relationship with the victim and that they'd had a fight prior to her death, but claimed that he loved her very much and that he had nothing to do with her murder. In fact, even though he worked at a voodoo shop, he barely even practiced it. It was more of just a passing interest he kept up to make sure he was keeping Marie happy.

The defense attorney went so far as to bring in a voodoo practitioner to testify on behalf of his client. The expert claimed that the victim's body was mutilated in the manner of a kimino, a ritual in voodoo that is designed to bring the dead back to the living. This was a practice someone like the boyfriend, a fellow named Gabriel LaPry would not have been equipped to even attempt. Still, the evidence was there and though they could not pin the murder itself on him, he served two years in prison. He'd been released a little over five months ago.

Upon reading this file, Palmer write down **KIMINO=resurrection?**

Thinking things over, Palmer ran a search for the two names of interest: Gabriel LaPry and Clarence Obo.

Obo was ruled out easily enough; earlier in the year, his body had been found in a swamp twenty miles outside of the city with two bullet holes in his head. The timing of it all meant that he would also have been eliminated from the string of earlier murders that seemed to be linked to the current ones.

That left Gabriel LaPry. He searched through the precinct records and found only an address. No phone number, no career history.

Palmer thought about calling the field office to get more information but thought that with a man like LaPry, an address might be enough. He also had the address of the voodoo shop where LaPry had worked prior to his girlfriend's death.

He got up, put on his jacket, and hurried out of the precinct. He grabbed a car and started on his way, heading out of the city and into the outskirts. And as he ventured out to find Gabriel LaPry, he found himself wishing Agent Grace was with him. Something about seeking out a man that was associated with voodoo and a murder charge felt a little dangerous, especially when heading for the less densely populated outskirts of the city.

Still, he put those fears to the side and continued on with that shadow of fear nipping at his heels.

***

The last known address of Gabriel LaPry was out near Cane Bayou, a stretch of grimy river that fed into Lake Pontchartrain. The property was a good distance off of the central paved roads, winding back into a series of non-state maintained roads that the visitors never saw and locals pretended did not exist.

The plot of land wasn't the sort of swampy land that non-Louisianan pictures in their mind, but it wasn't too far removed. The small driveway Palmer drove down was nothing more than a dirt track. And from the looks of the grass growing in the center and along the edges, it had not been used in quite some time.

That's why he wasn't all that surprised to find the house vacant. The grass around it had grown wild and a healthy growth of kudzu had overtaken the left outer wall. When Palmer got out of his car and closed the door, the noise of it sent a flock of birds flying out of the partially caved-in screen porch.

Palmer uttered a curse when he accepted the fact that he'd wasted half an hour driving out here. It seemed like he may have to call up the bureau after all. Maybe they'd have a more up to date address.

He got back into the car and cut a U-turn in the tall grass. He meandered back down the dirt road, wondering if Agent Grace was having any luck on her end with Dr. Penderhook.

With his thoughts on Agent Grace, he just happened to spot a man out in his yard. He was crouched down on the ground, looking at the underside of a push-style lawn mower that he had tilted up on its side. As far as Palmer could tell, it was the only house between here and LaPry's old place.

Palmer stopped the car and parked in the center of the dirt road. He seriously doubted he'd be blocking any traffic. Slowly, he walked into the man's yard. He was an African American man of middle age. He wore a straw hat and was smoking a cigarette as he tightened the bolt around the mower blade.

"Sir? Excuse me...," Palmer said.

The man turned his head and nodded. "Saw you stop your car right there. You lost or something?"

He spoke with a slight French dialect, not quite Cajun but sure as hell not the smoother tones spoken through most of New Orleans.

"No, sir. I'm not lost. I'm an FBI agent. Agent Scott Palmer. I'm out this way because I was looking for a man by the name of Gabriel LaPry. You familiar with that name?"

The man chuckled and nodded. He carefully let the mower back down on its wheels and stood up. He wiped his hands on his well-worn jeans before taking another drag of his cigarette and flicking it carelessly out into his yard.

"Yeah, I know ol' Gabe. Fo' sure."

"You know when he moved out of his house?"

"Well, I don't know that he ever came back to it at all after he did that time in prison, you know."

"Do you know why he went to prison?"

"They say he killed his girlfriend. That creepy ass Cheri woman."

"Do you think he did it?"

The black man shrugged. It was a shrug that not only indicated he wasn't sure, but that he likely didn't care, either. "Who knows? I didn't think he seemed the type, but I didn't know the man well."

"What *do* you know about him?"

"Nothin'. He's a quiet man. Never said much. Never gave anybody trouble, neither. Didn't bother anyone. He didn't drink or smoke or nothing. Kept to himself."

"Is there anyone that would know more about him? Know where he might've moved to?"

The man shrugged again and shook his head. "I don't think so. He was a loner."

"Do you know where he went when he left here?"

"Naw. Somebody said he went to live with his brother out in Texas. I don't remember who told me that or when they told it. That was a few months ago. I think right around the time he was out of jail. He might be dead for all I know."

"You referred to his girlfriend as creepy. Did you know her at all?"

"Only from when she'd come around to visit him. She was big into the voodoo you know? Took that shit real serious."

"You ever talk with her?"

"Once. I was out frog gigging one night and bumped into her. She was just walking on down the road, chanting something. Creepy. Like I said. Oh, but don't you know...her brother showed up not too long after Gabriel went to prison. Came by here asking the same kinda stuff you're asking. I'm pretty sure he went into the house and stole some stuff."

Again, he shrugged.

"Is there anything else you can think of?"

"No. Sorry. I mind my own business, you know? It's why I live all the way out here."

Palmer nodded and looked around at the thick blanket of forest all around them. Just half an hour away from New Orleans proper and it was like a different world. It felt much hotter, too.

"Well, thank you for your time, sir."

"Sure, yeah."

And as if he had already forgotten about the conversation, he primed up his mower by the little gas bulb and went to cranking it. He had it going by the time Palmer was in the car. A thick stream of exhaust rolled up into the air toward Palmer, as if escorting him right out of the woods and pushing him to the next stage of this case.

CHAPTER NINETEEN

When Camille sat down across from Dr. Albert Penderhook, she was stricken by his almost lackadaisical posture. He looked like a man about to hit the beach or watch a movie rather than a respected professor of anthropology. The top two buttons of his white button-down shirt were unbuttoned and his hair looked as if it had been out in the sun for a good amount of time. She guessed him to be about forty, but he was the sort of man that carried forty as if he was still living like he was twenty-one.

"I want to thank you for meeting with me this morning," Camille said. "As I said on the phone, Agent Scott Palmer thought you'd be of some assistance."

"Well, I'm happy to help if I can. On the phone, you said you think these murders you're working on might be voodoo related?"

"That's where I'm leaning, yes."

She handed him the single case file she'd compiled.

"There are crime scene photos in there, but they are very minimal. Just...well, I just want you to be warned."

He nodded his appreciation. While he looked at the files, Camille took a moment to study the office. It was both well-organized and slightly messy at the same time. It was the perfect mix of book-worm teenager and studious professor. There were volumes of books on a shelf on the right wall, holding volumes on ancient vocalizations and tribes, as well as books on psychedelic drugs. There were a number of artifacts and treasures on his desk and shelf, but it was all offset by one of those tacky-looking big-head toys called Pops. Penderhook's Pop was the likeness of Indiana Jones.

The photos didn't seem to bother Penderhook too badly. After he'd looked at all eight of them, he set them out on his desk in a way that they could both study them.

"How far apart were the locations they were found in?"

"Roughly twelve miles," Camille said. "As far as we can tell, there is no connection between the locations other than they were in the same large stretch of forest."

"Well, to me, the most interesting thing isn't so much that they were injected with something to knock them out."

"It's those pin prick marks on their chests, right?"

"Yes."

"Have you ever seen that before? Is it part of some sort of bizarre ritual I just haven't heard of?"

"Well, we *are* in voodoo territory here. But even if we weren't, I'd say there's SOME sort of ritualistic elements."

"So let's say I'm a newbie to this," Camille said. "Can you explain *why* you feel this way?"

"Well, the pinpricks themselves mean something. They're not random. And the circular formation of them indicate something recurring. Like a loop. And if you get into symbology for just about any culture or religion, that's often a sign or indicator of rebirth. And the fact that it's right there, on their chests, is even more interesting. But it's not any sort of voodoo I've ever seen or heard of being practiced in this area."

"What about other areas?"

"Well, I'm not sure if you know this, but the culture of voodoo originated in the Congo. I guarantee you that about seventy percent of the so-called practitioners around this area don't even know a lot of the deep-rooted Condo practices. The Congo traditions have been mixed with a lot of other cultural practices. Just like Louisiana has a Cajun culture, the Congo has a voodoo culture."

"OK, I get that. But what does it mean in regards to this case?"

"Voodoo practitioners, or bokors as we call them, have a lot of different ways of performing rituals. But there are a couple of things that are consistent. One of them is pin marks. You see, the bokors believed in a spiritual version of acupuncture. If a bokor wanted to gain the favor of some spirit, they'd use the marks to pin the spirit to their body."

"Any reason they'd choose the chest? I'd assumed it was because it's where the heart is." She tapped the photos and added: "But these marks aren't over the heart; they're right in the center of the chest."

"You've got me on that one, too. If I had to guess, though, it's because they're using it as the center of the body. The stomach, of course, would be the center. But on women, the center of the body is also where the womb resides. They could be avoiding the womb, maybe because of a respect of it. I don't really know."

He leaned forward and looked to the pictures again. With a slight frown on his face, he asked: "Do you know anything about the loa?"

"I've heard of them. Spooky stories, really, and nothing more. I grew up in the area."

"Ah," he said, as if it explained everything. "Well, in a nutshell, the loa are very real entities to anyone that seriously practices voodoo. Loa are spirits, essentially, that have powerful sway over the natural world, human behavior, and even fate. Some even believe them to be gods.

"Now, those pin pricks also remind me of another item often used to invoke the loa."

A light flickered in the back of her mind and Camille was embarrassed she'd not thought of it before. "A voodoo doll."

Penderhook nodded. "Right. The loa are compelled by ritual. This ritual utilizes the body in order to connect the living with the spiritual world of the loa."

"So based on all of this, you'd have no problem assuming these murders are centered around voodoo."

"I think it's a safe assumption. When we spoke on the phone, you said there were injection marks but no discernible drugs found in the bodies, right?"

"Correct."

"That makes me even more confident."

"Well, have you ever seen this before?"

"I can't say that I have. There are many different ritual symbols and presentations, even in the fact that they are displayed on these logs in the forest. But it's a strange mixture of different cultures and...well, I'd hate to guess at what the purpose is." A thoughtful and troubled look came over his face. "However...there was something in the news not too long ago. I doubt it garnered the interest if local PD and surely not the FBI..."

"What was it?"

"Local wildlife agencies and forestry organizations were finding animals in the forest. They were all pinned to stumps and in some cases, the heads were removed. Otters, foxes, owls. But they were stuck with numerous pins, as if they were living, breathing, voodoo dolls."

"Was it in this same stretch of forest?"

"Some of them, yes. But I think some were also out in the marshes. It went on for about six weeks, if I recall."

With the same thoughtful look on his face, he started typing something into the laptop on his desk. After clicking around and scrolling for about thirty seconds, he turned the computer around to her.

"Here it is. I didn't know if they even ended up finding the guy that did it."

Camille leaned closer to the screen and scanned the article Penderhook had pulled up for her. The article told the same story Penderhook had just told her. In the end, eighteen animals had been found but the man that had been charged for the crimes claimed there were easily fifty out there somewhere.

"Do you mind?" she asked, reaching for the laptop.

"Help yourself."

She did. She exited the article and then searched to see what had happened to the man responsible for the horrendous acts. His name was Gil Ledeaux. He'd gone to trial and had originally got eighteen months imprisonment for animal cruelty. Ledeaux bemoaned his religious freedoms and the eighteen months were reduced to three months and a small fine.

This had all occurred less than a year ago, meaning that Ledeaux was out and living his life.

It felt a bit like a stretch. But the inclusion of pins, pin marks, and being found pinned to stumps in the very same woods warranted at least a visit. If nothing else, perhaps Ledeaux could clue her in to some other voodoo approaches she and Penderhook had missed.

"Agent Grace, do you mind me asking how many girls have been killed this time?"

"Three so far. The latest of which was taken and killed last night."

"My God," he breathed. "Please do let me know if I can be of any further help."

"Oh, I think you've been plenty of help, Dr. Penderhook. And if you could print me copies of these two articles, I think I'll leave you to your day now."

Penderhook did so, and gladly. And while he pulled the papers from the printer behind his desk, Camille was already thinking of the sort of person it took to litter the forest with animals as a part of a religious sacrifice.

In her mind, the jump from that to the bodies she and Palmer were looking into wasn't a very big leap to make at all.

CHAPTER TWENTY

Anger is a gift.

He'd heard that somewhere but could not remember where. Maybe a poet or philosopher. Hell, maybe an old rock song for all he knew.

But he knew it to be true. He felt it in his bones as he lifted the old and weary table over his head. He slammed it down to the floor and watched it splinter into hundreds of nearly dry-rotted pieces.

Why hadn't it worked?

She should be back by now.

Obviously, he was doing something wrong. But what?

It came down to one of two things. Either he was choosing the wrong sorts of women to sacrifice or he was getting the location all wrong. He was quite certain that's why he'd failed the first time. He knew that the location had been all wrong. The energies had not been aligned and the spirits had been displeased.

Had he made that same mistake again?

If so, maybe it was a blessing in disguise. He couldn't strike in the French Quarter again. If he did, the cops were surely going to catch him. For goodness sake, he'd almost been busted with the last girl now, hadn't he?

So maybe he did need to switch up the location. Not only the location of the sacrifices but of his hunting grounds. This was tricky, though, as everything told him it needed to be done nearby. The city of New Orleans was meant to be the altar. But he needed to change things up. He needed to be safer. Smarter.

He let his anger come to the surface once more. He picked up one of the legs that had broken off of the end table and swung it into the cheap plasterboard walls of the shack he called a home. Putting a hole in the wall felt far too good.

Enjoying the release and the adrenaline of his anger, he sat down on the floor and thought things through. What did he need to do different?

He needed clarity to understand the answer to that. He could not let his emotions get the best of him. He took a series of deep breaths, closing his eyes and focusing on the weight and importance of his task.

Slowly, the anger in him began to fade. The frustration of being unable to get what he wanted to happen was slipping away and he was left with a nagging sense of doubt.

The doubt was worse than the anger.

It was a clawing sensation. An itch that he could not scratch but needed to. Bile began to rise in his throat and then, after one more moment of indecision, he began to shake with a sort of nervous excitement.

If he wanted her back, the sacrifices were necessary. He'd undergo a dozen more if that's what it took.

And slowly but surely, he was starting to understand that it may take that many more. It may take even more than that.

If so, that was fine. He'd do whatever was necessary.

And God help whoever tried to get in his way.

***

Seeking a new place for the ritual was almost like starting over. It was almost like going back to the drawing board. The girls along the French Quarter had been easy. Find a drunk and insecure one and you were made. And fortunately for him, that sort of young woman was fairly common in a busy city where appearance and status were everything.

But he left the city behind, driving his car away under a beautiful afternoon sun.

He'd been in this area all of his life. He'd studied the area and its people, its nooks and crannies. He knew where people were weak and in need.

The city had offered up the weak and vulnerable.

Ah, but the communities outside of the city, the communities that lived in its filthy shadow, many of them were both of those things, but they were also desperate.

As he neared the more rural areas outside of New Orleans, swamp and lush marshes at every turn, he started to wonder if he should have started out here to begin with. If he could find just one or two young women that had been traumatized by their daddy or were seeking the approval of *any* man, his job may turn out to be easier than he thought.

Yes, the French Quarter had been easier. And though the work may be harder out here in the sticks, he thought the fruit might be riper.

And if need be, he'd pluck from those vines until they were completely bare.

By the time he saw the first of what were many side roads off into the maze of greenery all around him, his anger was a thing of the past.

A smile touched his face.

This was the answer. This was the right path.

He'd have her back soon.

But first, there was much fruit to be plucked.

CHAPTER TWENTY ONE

On her way back out to her car in the visitor's lot, Camille placed a call to Palmer. He answered on the third ring, the echoing quality of the call indicating that he'd taken it over Bluetooth in the car.

"So your man Penderhook was a pretty big help," she said. "Thanks for that."

"Learn anything helpful?"

"Just more vindication that it's likely voodoo related. But I also sort of stumbled onto a potential lead. Does the name Gil Ledeaux mean anything to you?"

He thought about it for a moment before responding: "No. I don't think so. Should it?"

"He got caught sacrificing animals out in the woods in some pretty barbaric ways. Penderhook came up with a few theories that made me think it might be related. Palmer, I'm starting to wonder if the pin pricks on the chest are some sort of substitute for a voodoo doll. That these women are being used as a means to..I don't know...to maybe inflict some sort of punishment on someone else. And yes, as I say that out loud, I understand how flimsy it sounds."

"Flimsy, absolutely. But I think it might be down the right path, as much as I don't want to admit that."

"You know where this Ledeaux character is?" Camille asked.

"Give me a few seconds. I can make a call to the PD and try to get his contact info."

"Thanks. What about you? Anything new on your end?"

"Two leads," Palmer answered. "One went nowhere because the guy was murdered. The other is sort of still open. A dead address and no one seems to know where he went. He did some jail time and just seems to have disappeared. When I make your call, I'm going to dig up my info, too."

"Sounds good. Thanks for the help."

They ended the call just as she arrived at her car. She sat behind the wheel for a moment with no clear direction to go. She thought about the house that sat on a chunk of marshland about an hour south of here, land that contained the house she'd grown up in.

You know you're going to end up there, she thought. *Even if it's not until after this case is closed, you know you have to, right?*

"Shut up."

The remark was to no one in particular, but directed at her father. She hated the fact that old memories of him had so much power over her. She hated that she'd let one single man have such a hold on her life.

Closing her eyes, she tried to keep the memories away, but they came all the same. She saw her father, blood on his hands, standing in the hallway of their small backwoods home. She saw the shame in his eyes, saw the way he both hated himself but was proud of his morbid bravery.

Oh, Camille. My little girl. Why did you have to be so good?

She started the car, crushing the thought.

Her phone rang two minutes later before she was even off the campus grounds. It was Palmer, delivering quickly as he'd promised.

"It's odd," he said, "but we somehow have more information on this Ledeaux guy than we have on some murderers. I do believe lots of animals are better than most people, but still...maybe this is a bit much."

"What've you got."

"Two phone numbers, an address, and place of employment."

"Can you text it all over? Being the middle of the day, I'd assume he's probably at work."

"Can do."

"What about you?" she asked. "Any luck with your guy's info?"

"Not yet. The guy is pretty much a ghost or so it seems. In the meantime, do you want me to come help with your end?"

"Not necessary. It's a man that was mean to animals. I think I can handle it."

He chuckled and said, "Oh, I bet you can. Sending your info now."

He was again true to his word. He sent over an address and three numbers, one of which turned out to be the number to Gannett Construction, the place where Gil Ledeaux worked. She called it and was greeted by a cheerful sounding woman.

"This is Gannet Construction. Can I help you?"

"My name is Agent Camille Grace, with the FBI," she said, cutting right to the chase. "I'm looking for Gil Ledeaux."

"Oh, I'm sorry. This is the corporate offices. If you're looking for a contractor, I can get you their individual numbers."

99

"Actually, is there any way you can tell me if he's working a specific site? It would save a lot of time."

"You know what? I actually *can* do that. Hold on..."

Camille heard typing in the background for a few seconds before she was greeted with the friendly female voice again.

"Mr. Ledeaux is working on a retirement home remodel in the Garden District. Would you like the address?"

She had his cell number, which would do just fine. But she figured a face-to-face would be more effective. "Yes, that would be great."

The woman gave Camille the address, and she plugged it into her GPS. After ending the call, Camille followed the directions deeper into a city she had once known well.

But that same city was also starting to feel like a foreign world that had nothing for her but old memories that were still trying to lure her back to the pains of her past.

***

When she reached the site of the retirement home, she parked behind a row of Gannet Construction work trucks. She spotted two men that were looking over a series of plans and blueprints on the hood of one of the trucks. She approached them, knowing full well that her asking to speak to Ledeaux would draw suspicion toward him but she wasn't concerned about that.

They had three dead women on their hands and she'd be damned if she was going to let polite mannerisms slow her down. Still, she was subtle as she approached the truck and discreetly placed her ID on top of the blueprints.

"I need to speak to Gil Ledeaux," she said.

The man on the other side of the hood looked troubled for only a moment. But then he sighed, sized Camille up, and nodded toward the building.

"He's on the west side. Can't miss him. He's the idiot with the kudzu vine tattooed all the way down his right arm."

"Thanks."

She put her ID away and walked across the retirement home lawn, angling over to the western edge. As it came into view, she saw a team of five men at work. Two were putting up the frame to a small half wall. Two others were aligning boards to make another section of the frame. Then, off to the side, there was a man cutting a two-by-four with a skill saw. An elaborate tattoo of a green vine ran down the length of his right arm.

She approached him and waited for him to run the saw through the board before she spoke.

"Mr. Gil Ledeaux?"

He wheeled around and gave her a surprised looked. "Yeah?"

He smiled thinly, making no effort to hide that he was checking her out. He was slightly muscular but had a bit of a gut on him. He was handsome in a resigned and somewhat grizzled sort of way, but there was something in his eyes that tilted it all. Right away, Camille could tell he was a man that kept secrets, a man that sought out trouble and controversy.

"I'm Agent Camille Grace, FBI. I need to ask you some questions."

"Ah, shit. About those damned animals?"

"In part."

"Look, I already got punished for that."

"Are you still doing those sorts of things?"

"Not that it's any of your business, but no."

"Are you still practicing voodoo?"

He sneered a bit here and looked over to the other workers. It was clear that he was uneasy talking about this around them. "No, not really. I'm not a pagan these days."

"And what does that mean, exactly?"

"It just means that I'm not interested in it anymore. I'm done with all that voodoo shit."

"Because it got you arrested?"

"Partly, yeah. Look, can you just tell me why you're here? I've been on the straight and narrow ever since I got out."

"How long has that been? Like five months?"

"In fact, yes." He was getting angry now. She could see it in the set of his jaw and the way the muscles in his arms were tightening. It almost made the tattooed kudzu appear as if it was moving.

"I do need to know about what you did to those animals. Was it part of some sort of ritual?"

"In a way," he said, barely even moving his mouth now. It was more like an irritated hissing coming through his teeth. "But I'm not going to talk about that."

"I'd appreciate it if you would. Mr. Ledeaux; I'm working a case where three young women have been killed. And there are markings on their bodies that are quite similar to what you did to those animals. The

101

fact that the bodies were discovered in the same forest doesn't make the whole thing—"

"That's not me anymore, I said! Look...when I was in prison, I understood what I'd done. And I understood the darkness of voodoo and how it corrupts. I found the Lord when I was in jail. I pray to Jesus now. He's the only one who can forgive me for the time I spent in all that darkness."

Camille didn't buy it—not all of it, anyway. It all went back to those shifty eyes. She hated the feeling of not trusting someone at first glance, but she got that feeling from Ledeaux.

"I can understand that. But I need you to come with me and tell me about that darkness. Even if you truly don't practice it anymore, any information you can give us will—"

"Sorry, but no."

She stepped closer and, in a soft voice, added: "Let's not make a scene in front of your co-workers."

"And if I say no?"

"Then I break out the handcuffs."

She saw the rage come into his face. It came like a wave, out of nowhere and crashing to the surface of his eyes.

"Hey man, go to hell!" he wailed.

He threw the end of the board he'd just sawed at her. She wheeled away from it but the edge of it still caught her along the upper arm.

To her surprise, he was coming at her again.

He had a hammer in his hand. He drew it back and was aiming it at her head.

The sudden explosion of violence had taken her off guard. This was no way to respond to a simple line of questioning. So, either he was lying through his teeth or something about his supposed former practice of voodoo had triggered him.

Whatever the case, she was going to have to kick his ass.

She sidestepped the blow easily and when he followed through, Camille threw out a well-placed jab that connected squarely with the side of his head. He stumbled, but not much.

The four men around them had scattered, leaving the two of them alone. One of them seemed to be running toward the lawn, maybe to get the foreman.

Ledeaux came rushing at her again, drawing the hammer back once more.

He let out a yell that was part anger and part frustration as he swung the hammer down again. He was so fueled with fury that his movements were very predictable. She ducked and moved hard to the left side. When she did, she swiveled out in a half-turn, sweeping her right leg across. She took his feet out from under him, and he went down hard.

He struck the very same board he's thrown at her. The hammer went clattering to the ground as Camille followed up her attack. Moving so fast that it was nearly all one fluid motion, she delivered an open-handed strike to Ledeaux's solar plexus, flipped him over, and pulled his hands behind his back. She then planted her knee in his lower back and slapped her handcuffs on him.

From the leg sweep to clicking the cuffs closed, only four seconds had passed.

As she reached down and roughly helped Ledeaux to his feet, she couldn't help the smart-ass comment that came out of her mouth.

"I don't believe Jesus would have approved of that."

He grunted and fought, but only slightly.

"I didn't do nothing."

"Before or after you threw the board at me and then came after me with a hammer. You just turned a line of basic questioning into an arrest for assault against a federal agent."

Ledeaux said nothing. Not as the other workers looked at him, not as she led him past the foreman and the work trucks, and not as she guided him into the back seat.

With her arm sore and bruising from the board strike, Camille backed away from the renovated retirement home as Ledeaux started to whimper like a scolded child in the back seat.

Camille didn't know if it was from guilt or the sudden reaffirming of his past sins and she really didn't care. Not now, anyway.

He'd have plenty of time to explain himself in an interrogation room. This time, without a hammer.

CHAPTER TWENTY TWO

Something about the abandoned condition of Gabriel LaPry's house still wasn't sitting right with Palmer. He chewed over it while he sat alone in his car in a convenience store parking lot.

If LaPry knew he was leaving town, why not try to sell the house? It would give him a little cushion of money to escape to wherever he had in mind. The only reason Palmer could think of was because selling the house would create something of an unnecessary paper trail. There would be forms and phone numbers, people that had interacted with him on occasion.

But by leaving it in his name, abandoned, well, that would be advantageous. First of all, the derelict nature of the place would instantly make people come to the same conclusion he and the mower-repairing neighbor had come to: that LaPry had skipped town.

But Palmer also knew that a house in LaPry's name, still standing in a familiar location, would give him a place to crash when he had nowhere else to go. And without the official trail of real estate agency involvement, LaPry essentially became a ghost.

This all made Palmer feel certain that LaPry hadn't gone far. Hell, for all he knew, Gabriel LaPry might still be in Louisiana.

He took out his phone, knowing that it could be nothing more than a distraction to follow this LaPry trail. But at the same time, it wasn't like they were drowning in leads.

He pulled up a name he called from time to time, when he needed information from the bureau fast—which often meant it came from unofficial channels. It had always worked though, and he had learned that under-the-table relationships in the bureau were typically much more effective than the regular channels. And this certain friend was something of an anarchist at heart, so he was okay doing favors under the table if it sped up the process and highlighted the bureau's often lagging response times.

The call was answered on the second ring. Palmer smiled a bit at the familiar warmth and humor in Patrick Belmont's voice.

"Is this the ineffable Agent Palmer?" Patrick asked.

"It is. You miss me?"

"Not really. Though digging for information for you *does* make me feel like a bit of a rebel. That *is* why you're calling, right?"

"Yes, it is. I need to find anything you have on a guy named Gabriel LaPry. Records will show in Louisiana not too long ago. Did some jail time. A current address or phone number would be great."

"One second. Let me work my magic."

What followed was about thirty seconds of tapping keys, then typing in another word, more tapping, and then some more typing.

"Got him," Patrick said, sounding pleased.

"You're a wonder," Palmer said.

"I am, aren't I?" Patrick replied, then grew a bit more serious. "So, I've got an address, but it's reading as vacant. All mail delivered there is being returned. It's been defunct for over a year now. I do have a phone number, though. And from what I can tell, it's currently active."

"That's great. And I suppose you know what my next question is going to be."

"I think I do. And you're going to have to wait a second. I'm sort of in the office. Why can't you just go through regular channels on this?"

"Because I don't have the time to wait. I've got a few dead girls here in New Orleans and don't have time to waste."

"Roger that. Hold on." Patrick was whispering now and then things went quiet for about thirty seconds.

"Okay, so the phone is active," he said quietly, "and I'm running a trace on it right now."

"You're like a magician."

"Wizard. Get it right. Now...you're in New Orleans, right?"

"Yes, I am."

"Huh. What a coincidence. So is this phone."

"No shit?"

"None whatsoever," Patrick said. "I'm running the location now to see where it is...and...well, it's actually just a bit outside of the city. The address is..." The sound of rapid-fire typing could be heard for a moment before Patrick finished his statement. "A bar called Cork's."

"Can you text me the address? And then maybe keep an eye on the phone and notify me again if it moves?"

"Will do. But we know how this works. Someone sitting at a bar just a bit after noon? I doubt they're going anywhere anytime soon."

"Thanks for this, Patrick."

"Oh, for sure. I'm keeping tabs. You owe me a shit-ton of beers the next time we all get together."

"Noted."

Palmer ended the call and when Patrick sent the text, he plugged it into his GPS. From what he saw, the drive would take about twenty-five minutes.

Feeling as if he were on a clock, Palmer pulled out of the convenience store lot, wondering if Camille was making as much progress as he was.

***

Cork's was located just close enough to the edge of town to still be consider part of New Orleans. it sat on the corner of a block that didn't seem to have much else going for it aside from a sketchy-looking barber shop.

Palmer walked inside, not having received a text from Patrick telling him that the phone had moved.

The place was small and dimly lit, the sort of bar you came to when you planned on either getting obliterated or were meeting with someone you were ashamed of. There were only six people at the bar, including a bartender that looked as if he'd rather be anywhere other than at work.

Having no idea what Gabriel LaPry looked like, Palmer figured he'd take the easiest route possible. He walked over to the bar, sat down at the right side, and ordered a drink from the bartender. He was a big man, the sort where it was hard to tell if there was some added cushion beneath his shirt or if it was mostly muscle. When he handed Palmer his beer, Palmer noticed a tattoo of a lizard along the back of the man's right hand.

Palmer sipped from the beer for a moment, eyeing the other five patrons, all sitting to his left.

"Gabriel LaPry." He spoke the name as if he were a teacher calling attendance.

Everyone looked in his direction, but only one of them seemed to be genuinely confused. It was an African American man of about thirty-five or so. He looked tired and was quite thin. He was wearing an old Saints tank-top and a pair of dingy cargo shorts.

When Palmer locked eyes with him, the man turned away, giving all of his attention to the beer bottle sitting in front of him.

Under his breath, Palmer said: "So it's going to be like that?"

He took another two sips of his beer and then got up from his stool. He carried the beer with him as he approached Gabriel LaPry.

"Mr. LaPry, there's a booth over there in the corner. Let's go have a drink together, yeah?"

The man looked at him and though he was trying to come off as tough, Palmer easily saw the uncertainty in the man's eyes.

"Nah, man, I don't swing that way."

"Oh, I don't either. And if I did, you would not be my type. No, I want to ask you some questions about that house you left abandoned."

"What? Nah man, you got the wrong person."

"That deer in the headlights look you gave me when I called out your name says otherwise."

"Who the hell are you, anyway?" LaPry asked, his eyes locked on his beer bottle.

"I'm an FBI agent. And I can make this real ugly for you if you don't—"

LaPry moved quickly for a scrawny guy. He didn't necessarily strike out and hit Palmer with his bottle, but he sort of tossed it at him. It was really only meant as a means of distraction, and it worked. By the time Palmer caught the bottle and had beer splashed up on his chest, LaPry was off of his barstool and rushing for the door.

"What the hell?" the bartender yelled, reaching under the bar for a weapon.

"No need," Palmer said, flashing his ID as he took off after LaPry.

When he stepped out into the street again, it was easy to locate LaPry. He was dashing hard to the right, heading down the sidewalk with his battered Crocs slapping like gunshots. More aggravated than anything else, Palmer ran after him.

LaPry took a hard right at the end of the block, rushing across an old, abandoned construction site. He leaped over a fallen board that had been placed cock-eyed against a fallen sawhorse. This little move proved to be his downfall.

He stumbled and nearly fell. By the time he'd gotten his feet back under him properly, Palmer had caught up to him. He reached out, grabbed the man's arm, and easily dodged the flailing punch LaPry dished out.

A simple leg-sweep took LaPry to the ground. As Palmer rested a knee in the man's back and applied his handcuffs, LaPry didn't bother fighting.

"You're Gabriel LaPry, yes?"

107

"Yeah."

"Why'd you lie?"

"Cuz the only people that would be looking for me are people I wouldn't want to see."

"Well, you're right about that. You're under arrest Mr. LaPry. I was only wanting to speak to you, but you sort of escalated that."

As he helped LaPry to his feet, he regarded Palmer with angry eyes. He'd also busted his lip during his fall to the ground.

"Why you need to talk to me anyway?"

"Just some run-of-the-mill questions about voodoo and some people you used to associate with. You got a problem with that?"

But LaPry said nothing else as Palmer walked him back to the street. A few people were watching them from the doorway of the Cork. LaPry hung his head low, and Palmer did his best to figure out if it was from embarrassment or rapidly approaching guilt.

CHAPTER TWENTY THREE

Ellie knew she was lucky to have a job but God, did she hate it. She was twenty-two, knew she had a killer body, and knew there were certain other things she could be doing to make money, but no...she was stuck here at the Quick-Go gas station. It was the only gas station and so-called convenience store for another ten miles or so, but they never got any traffic. She knew the management had been preparing to shut down for about a year now and it made perfect sense to her. She'd been on shift for three hours now and a grand total of five people had come in.

She knew what the Quick-Go's bread and butter was, though. The bulk of customers came in late at night, just before eleven o' clock, when the Quick-Go closed. Locals would by lots of beer and malt liquor for backwoods parties, miniature Mardi Gras get-downs out in the woods.

But she never saw any of that action. Nope, she was always given first shift. She knew why and appreciated it; her boss didn't want her working when drunk and loud guys came in late at night.

She supposed she should be grateful. She was getting paid just a bit above minimum wage to sit on her cute ass and read magazines while waiting for the next daytime customer to come in. It was usually lottery scratchers or some lost tourist asking for directions. The Quick-Go was pretty much an island, as only one road came in and out. That meant that, as she often thought, the only people who would come to this run-down place were people who REALLY knew the area or tourists that had somehow taken a wrong turn, driving about thirty miles the wrong way as they tried to reach New Orleans.

She finished up a copy of PEOPLE that was three months old and placed it back in the magazine rack. When she did, she noticed the old Buick rolling up to the gas pumps outside.

The driver got out slowly. He was an older gentleman, probably in his early fifties. His hair was white and thin. He was wearing dark jeans and a dressy jacket over a tee shirt.

"Hmmm," Ellie mumbled as she watched him walk to the pumps.

The Buick was one of those old models, but it looked in pretty good shape. It was waxed and clean, and Ellie could tell the rims were recently polished. The windows were tinted, so she couldn't see inside.

She watched the man place the gas nozzle into his car and then looked for another magazine to read. No one ever came in for gas anymore. It was all on credit cards or Apple Pay now.

She had just settled back down behind the counter when the little bell over the door sounded out. Apparently, she was wrong. The man in the jeans and the nice-looking jacket over his tee shirt had come inside. He had an apologetic and almost embarrassed look on his face as he shuffled over to the counter.

Ellie checked the pump dials and saw that he hadn't pumped anything yet.

"Everything okay?" Ellie asked.

"I suppose," the man said. He had a southern accent, but it was the charming sort, not the sort that instantly made her think the person speaking wasn't intelligent. "Everything seems okay out there, but there's just no gas coming out. And there's a reading on the screen that has some gibberish about an error code."

"What?"

Ellie had never heard of this before. She nearly told him to just pull ahead to the next pump but then remembered that it was out of order. The gas people wouldn't be out for another two days to repair it, either.

"Yeah, I thought it was weird, too," the man said.

Sighing, Ellie stepped out from behind the counter and walked the door. If both gas pumps were shut down, the Quick-Go's only purpose would be late night beer. And that meant the place would certainly not last much longer. She was going to have to take a look at this error message, take a picture of it, and send it to her boss.

She approached the pump, the man following a respectful distance behind. She stared at the pump for a moment, not understanding. Was this old bastard trying to prank her? Was he trying to—

He came up behind her with eerie speed. His arm went around her neck and she felt his power right away. It was deceptive and did not fit at all with his physical appearance.

"Ooh, hell no!"

Ellie jacked her head back hard. She felt the back of her head collide with the man's chin. He let out a surprised shout and Ellie was able to slip away. She started dashing back for the store, already mapping out her strategy. She'd lock the door, call the cops, and get the asshole's license plate number as he drove off.

She reached the door, reached for it and her fingers had nearly gripped the handle when he slammed into her from behind. Her head went slamming into the glass door, causing it to crack. He then grabbed her by the hair and she tried to fight, but the grip around her neck was just too strong. His other arm, his left, was busy with something else and it took her a while to understand what he was doing.

He had a knife. He was going to stab her, gut her like a fish in the parking lot of the Quick-Go. A shitty way to die, for sure.

She realized just a bit too late that he wasn't going to stab her at all, .not in the traditional sense, anyway. He jabbed her with something. A needle, maybe. Yeah, a needle. She could see the syringe as he yanked it away.

"Hey, what," she said. "What are you—"

But he was already leading her away from the Quick-Go, back towards his Buick. She tried to fight but it felt like she was moving underwater. All she could feel was him and the gentle sting where he'd injected her.

That didn't last long, though. He opened the back door and when he started to lay her down into the back seat, he rammed her head against the door frame. He did it hard and with great intention.

Rockets of pain flared in Ellie's head and just before she blacked out, she morbidly wondered if things were this dangerous on night shift.

CHAPTER TWENTY FOUR

Camille stood in front of Gil Ledeaux, arms folded and sizing the man up. it was quite obvious that being in an interrogation room didn't bother him. The only emotion he showed at all was something similar to anger. Maybe some embarrassment, too, seeing as how an unsuspecting woman had kicked his ass in front of a few men he worked with.

"Back at the construction site, you said you'd changed your ways in prison," she said. "So can you look back on what you did to those animals in the woods and tell me WHY you did it."

Now a bit of shame crept into his expression. It was a genuine reaction, so genuine that Camille almost regretted asking him about it.

"Because I thought it was expected of me. It wasn't just plain voodoo, the basic shit everyone in New Orleans pretends to just accept and be interested in. I got in with some wrong people. Some bad stuff."

"Like what?"

His jaw clenched a bit, an indicator that he might be on the verge of getting emotional. She supposed it made sense. If he'd lashed out at her without much thought back at the construction site, it *did* point to a man that was prone to emotional outbursts.

"Like black magic."

"And the animals you nailed to trees were part of it?"

"Yes. Part of the rituals."

"That's why I came looking for you, Mr. Ledeaux. I need to know some of those details. We're looking at three dead women, killed in the same woods you performed those rituals, exposed on stumps and logs the same way you set our your animals."

Ledeaux shook his head. "I never killed a human. Not a single time. Cut myself here and there for blood-letting, but nothing like murder."

"I'll take your word for that for now," Camille said. But really, she was still skeptical. Sometimes she got gut feelings about people and she was having one now that told her Ledeaux was just bad news, plain and simple. "But still, tell me about the rituals with the animals."

"It's not like it sounds," he said. "It's a classical African art known as Santeria. It started in the Caribbean, I think, and spread to New

Orleans. Learned about it when I was in prison for the first time, and the people I met there were quick to tell me about it."

"The first time?" Camille asked. "What were you in prison for?"

"Assault."

"How many times have you been in prison?"

"Too many."

"Tell me about the ritual with the animals."

"It involves sacrifice. It's a way to appease the orishas, the spirits." He shook his head and she no longer saw the violent man that had attacked her less than an hour ago. "And I'd love to tell you that now that I have the Lord, I know it's all nonsense. But I saw and experienced things that...well, I know it's all real. And that was too damned scary for me."

"Who were you performing these rituals for?"

"Myself, but under the guidance of a priestess."

"What priestess?"

"A woman named Odessa. She's dead, though. Murdered while I was in prison."

"Mr. Ledeaux, if I ask you where you've been over the course of the last four or five days, would you have clear alibis? Days and nights."

He thought it over and nodded. "Yeah. I was at a Bible study two of the last four nights. At home the other two."

"Any proof?"

"Not unless you count having Chinese food delivered as proof."

Camille said nothing but knew that they could indeed use food delivery as proof. She also figured the Bible study could be used as an alibi if anyone would vouch for him. She studied him a moment longer and nodded almost appreciatively to him.

"I swear...I know nothing about any murders."

She believed him, but didn't dare say such a thing. "An officer will be in soon to work with you on checking your alibis," she said. "And just a heads up, you're going to be charged with the attempted assault of a federal agent."

With that, Camille left the room without gauging his reaction. She walked out into a wide hallway, feeling out of place in a precinct she'd never been in before. As she headed for the bullpen area, she stopped just shy of the end of the hallway when she saw Agent Palmer coming around the corner and along the edge of the bullpen. He had a man with him, in handcuffs and bleeding slightly from the lip.

113

Palmer said something to an officer as he passed and the officer nodded. He grabbed a set of keys from a nearby desk and escorted Palmer directly toward Camille.

"Who do we have?" Camille asked as Palmer and his suspect passed her in the hallway.

"Gabriel LaPry. History of violence against Creoles, namely tied up in the murder of a woman, a murder that seemed to have been heavily influenced by voodoo practices. Attempted to disappear off the radar after he served some time in prison, though he didn't do a very good job. He stayed right around New Orleans." Palmer grinned and said, "Want to join me?"

She followed Palmer and the officer to the interrogation room directly beside Ledeaux's.

She watched as Palmer led LaPry into the single chair that sat behind the dingy-looking table. The room, like Ledeaux's, was rather bright and smelled of disinfectant.

"Want to tell me why you ran when I asked about your house?" Palmer asked.

"I told you. Anyone that knew me when I lived at that house isn't someone I want to talk to."

"So you tried escaping your old life but only went about fifteen miles down the road. Is that it?"

"I know people around here," LaPry said. "Born and raised. It's home."

"You ever crash at your old place when times got tough?"

"Yeah, a few times."

Palmer gestured to Camille and said, "Mr. LaPry, this is Agent Grace. She knows nothing about your history. I'd really love it if you told her what led to the murder of Marie Cheri."

LaPry sneered, the blood form his lips glistening in the bright light. "You probably know more than me on that one. I didn't kill her, and I don't know who did."

"But you dated her, right? You knew she was into voodoo."

"Yeah, and?"

"Don't you have theories?"

He eyed both agents with scorn and allowed himself a nervous chuckle. "Yeah, I have a few."

"I'd like to hear them."

"I think she was into some stuff she shouldn't have been." He said it quickly, as if he wanted the words out of his mouth as fast as possible. He closed his eyes and let the words sink in.

"What kind of stuff?" Palmer asked.

LaPry stared at the table, trying to think. "I think something bad happened in her apartment. I think someone killed her. I think she brought something home with her. Something evil. She'd bring shit in the apartment sometimes and I'd just feel it, you know?"

"Please don't tell me you think *evil* killed her," Palmer said.

"No. I think someone killed her *for* the evil thing. Whatever it was. The thing is, she WAS killed in a ritualistic manner, but it was like a mix of weird practices."

"And the reports say you never really practiced, right?"

"Right. I just sort of pretended to keep Marie happy."

"And it was a good relationship?"

"Yeah. The cops only tried pinning it on me because they didn't have any answers. You should know this if you're a cop around here. If voodoo is involved, they wrap that shit as quick as they can: make excuses, sweep it under the rug, whatever it takes." He eyed them suspiciously, studying them. "What's this about, anyway?"

Camille couldn't tell if Palmer intended to tell him or not. It didn't matter, either way; a knock at the door broke the moment apart. The same officer that had led Palmer and Camille to this room poked his head in.

"Sorry to interrupt," he said. "But it looks like we've got another one."

CHAPTER TWENTY FIVE

Even before they reached the location where the body was found, Camille knew this one was different. She was certain Palmer knew it, too. It was evident in the fact that the location was taking them out of the city. They were currently driving down a two-lane road, shadowed by over-hanging trees. New Orleans was a good fifteen miles behind them now.

"So we think it's a good thing or a bad thing that he's moving outside of the city?" Palmer asked from behind the steering wheel.

"No clue. I don't even know if it's far enough to claim it's a sign of him moving. Maybe he could have just struck when it was convenient."

"Maybe," Palmer said, though Camille wasn't sure if he bought it.

They sat in thick silence as Palmer turned off the two-lane road and onto a thin strip of gravel track. A sign to the right read: END STATE MAINTENANCE 0.6. Looking ahead, Camille thought she could see settling dust from several cars passing down the gravel over the past half an hour or so.

When the road came to an end, they found two State Police cars already parked in the oval-shaped turnaround spot. As they got out of the car, Camille could already see the police blues through the trees. They weren't moving but standing still. Apparently, the body wasn't carried as deeply out into the woods this time.

She wasn't quite sure what it meant, but she thought it could mean the killer felt hurried this time. It made her wonder how fresh this kill was.

Camille and Palmer rushed through the grove of trees and joined the three policemen. They were in a sort of semi-circle around a stump. It was much smaller than the ones that came before. Camille couldn't help but wonder if this might mean something, too. Maybe he HAD been hurried. Maybe he WAS scared.

Even if she didn't know that they were in a different section of forest, many miles away from the other murders, she would have sensed the change in the environment. Something about this strip of forest just felt different.

Camille stepped forward to join the semi-circle of policemen. They all had their hands behind their backs and were looking down at a stump.

"Who found her?" Camille asked, the second she was close enough to not have to shout.

"Kid with his dog," one of the officers said. He had his arms locked behind his back and was looking at the stump, but his head was dipped backward so he could look at her. "He was out hunting squirrels and came across her."

"Look," Camille said. "There's blood on her head. That's different."

"Bruising, too," one of the officers said.

"FRESH bruising," Palmer clarified. "Jesus, this had to have happened recently. Like within the last few hours."

"Her name is Ellie Myers," one of the three officers said.

"How do you know?" Camille asked.

"Not too long before the call about the body came in, we got a call from a fella that owns a convenience store about seven miles east of here. Said he was trying to get in touch with a cashier of his and she wasn't answering the phone. An officer went by to check it out and found some cracked glass along the door. Door was unlocked and everything."

Camille hated to leave a crime scene so quickly but everything in her gut, every instinct and every bit of training told her they needed to be at that convenience store. If the killer had taken his usual precautions here at the ritual site, there would be few clues.

But if they could check out the site of where he captured this young woman so recently, maybe there would be something.

"Convenience stores have cameras," Scott pointed out.

"What's it called?" Camille asked.

"The Quick-Go. Right down the road. The only thing worth even stopping by for a few miles. You can't miss it. The cop cars that are parked there will help, too."

Camille nodded, though she took a moment to look over the body of Ellie Myers. She deserved at least that much.

Aside from the drying blood around a small laceration on her forehead—right by the bruising—she was just as unblemished as the other victims. She leaned in close to inspect the area above the left hip and saw the irritated redness there. She'd been injected very recently. Upon inspecting the chest she also saw the little bumps between the breasts.

117

"Do you have an ETA on forensics?" she asked the officers, her voice soft and trembling with anger and frustration.

"En route as we speak. Maybe five minutes."

"Keep us posted," she said, already turning back toward the woods and their car. "We'll be at the convenience store."

With Scott behind her, Camille marched quickly back toward their car, fueled by the notion that the killer may have covered this ground as recently as two hours ago.

***

The cop had been right: the Quick-Go stood out quite easily among the sprawled woodland outside of New Orleans. Camille found this especially odd considering that the place looked as if it had been overlooked for countless years. Dusty, in need of maintenance, and encompassed by swampy-looking trees and brush, it was the sort of place most people probably only stopped by for gas or to use the bathroom.

When they arrived, there were two cop cars in the lot. One was parked lengthwise by one of the two entrances, to let any travelers know that now was not the time to stop. The other was parked in front of the building in a similar position.

Inside, two uniformed officers were speaking to an overweight man with a beard badly in need of a trim. He looked genuinely upset as he spoke to the police. When he saw Camille and Palmer enter, a look of gratitude flashed across his face but was quickly overtaken by sadness.

The two cops also had looks of relief on their faces as Camille showed her FBI ID.

"Agents Grace and Palmer," she recited.

"Already been out to the site where the body was found?" one of the cops said.

"Yes. But we feel like there are more answers to be found here."

"Need us to stick around?"

"If you want. Maybe have a look around the parking lot. Tire tracks, footprints, anything like that."

The cops nodded, both seeming to savor the idea of getting outside. Four bodies in a week...Camille was sure they were all on edge and while they wanted answers, the presence of the FBI took a great deal of that burden off of their shoulders.

"FBI, huh?" the overweight man said. "Is it that serious?"

118

"It is," Palmer said. "There have been three others found just like Ellie Myers."

"I can tell you're upset," Camille said. "But time is of the essence here. I see a camera right there behind the counter. Is that the only one you have on the premises?"

"No. There's one outside, too, but it's not the best. I've been meaning to upgrade, but it's just too damned expensive, even with the fly-by-night companies."

"We need to see the footage from the past hour or so. Can you do that?"

"Absolutely," he said. "Come on back behind here."

Camille and Palmer joined the man behind the counter. As he led them to the far left side, a little corner hidden by a display of snack cakes and twelve packs of soda, he offered his hand to both of them.

"Name's Duncan Miller. I run the place and knew Ellie really well. I never let her run this place during the night because I was worried about her but...well, then this happened. Day, night, doesn't matter apparently. People are just cruel no matter the time of day apparently."

Miller sat down on a ratty little stool that groaned under his weight. A small monitor sat in front of him, giving the same live view from three different points within the store. He used a mouse sitting on the backside of the counter to pull up a menu and then navigated around a bit until the screen flickered and took them back three hours in time.

"There's Ellie," Miller said, frowning.

Camille looked to the screen and saw the girl wiping down the counter by the register. She then plucked a magazine out of the rack at the lower end of the counter and took her position behind the register.

"Is it always this dead in here?" Palmer asked.

"Most of the time."

"Mr. Miller, can you track forward a bit?" Camille asked. "Not so fast that we'll miss something, but fast enough so we don't need to watch every fly or mote of dust that passes."

"Yeah, one second."

Miller operated the computer for a few minutes and they watched Ellie move in a perky-jerky fashion. Camille watched Ellie pass the time by putting her hair behind her ears, reading her magazine, and glancing at her phone on occasion.

After another minute or so, Ellie got up and replaced the magazine. She then looked out of the window for a moment.

"Stop it right here," Camille said.

He did and just a few moments later, someone came into the store. From what Camille could tell, it was a man. He was walking slowly and looking at the floor. It was odd, but his posture made it seem like he was walking like an embarrassed child, afraid to make eye contact. There was nothing immediate about it that seemed threatening or suspect.

She felt herself go cold for a moment as she realized she could very well be looking at their killer. She stared at the shape on the screen, as if trying to draw more information from that grainy image.

The man and Ellie spoke for about twenty seconds before the man turned and walked out. To their surprise, Ellie followed.

"What the hell?" Palmer said.

They sat there and watched the empty store for another minute or so.

"Fast forward again," Palmer said.

Miller did as he was asked. Within seconds, it became clear that Ellie was not coming back in."

"So he said something that convinced her to go outside," Camille said. "What reasons would she have in terms of her job to go outside?"

"None," Miller said.

"Okay, let's try the outside camera."

Miller nodded and clicked around a bit. "I apologize in advance for the terrible quality."

Camille saw what he meant right away.

The image was blurry, dark, and barely visible. The only thing they could see clearly were the gas pumps.

A car was parked in front of the pumps. It was an older model Buick. Already, as the man and Ellie approached the car, their shapes were blurry and ill-defined.

"Yeah, this quality sucks," Palmer said.

They continued to watch. Ellie went to the pumps and looked at something. As she did, the man moved swiftly, belying any hint that he'd been slow or somehow feeble when he'd come into the store. They watched the attack and Ellie's near escape. But in the end, he carried her back to the car without much fight.

"Rewind a bit," Camille said.

Miller did and within a few seconds, Camille stopped him.

"Right there," she said. "Jesus he's fast."

"I saw it, Palmer said. "He injected her with something, right in the hip."

They watched the man haul her into the back of his car. Not once did he face the camera, and Camille was quite certain he did it all on purpose.

"My God," Miller said, his hand to his mouth.

They watched the car leave, the camera's quality far too poor to make out a clear license plate.

"You think the State PD has the equipment to somehow make out that plate?" Camille asked.

"I can find out," Palmer said. "I'll shoot it over to the field office, too."

Camille couldn't stop the almost childish response. She slammed her hand down on the counter in frustration. "Damn it!"

They'd been so close. The killer's car had been *right there* and they still somehow had nothing.

They were running blind again and with another head start of an hour or more on them, the killer could be anywhere by now. But she knew what her next step was, and she was not looking forward to it. She and Palmer were going to have to go speak to freshly grieving parents and sometimes, in her experience, that was even harder than staring a killer in the face.

CHAPTER TWENTY SIX

Camille looked up to the small, cozy house and sighed. There was already a cop car in the driveway, so the hard part had already been done. Some other poor officer of the law had broken the news to the Myers family. Now all she and Palmer had to do was try to question a newly grieving set of parents.

"Were you ever good at this part of it?" Palmer asked her.

"I don't know. I mean, how do you get good at something like this? Questioning parents that just lost their child...it's awful."

"It is." He shrugged and added, "So let's go ahead and get it done."

The Myers home was located in a small subdivision fifteen miles away from the Quick-Go. It was an older neighborhood, so there were sizable yards with some trees and room for flower beds, but the houses were very middle-of-the-road. As they walked up the faded, cracked sidewalk, Camille looked to the forest that bordered the backside of the property.

It did not escape her that coming out this way, even further away from the city, brought her closer to the house where she'd grown up. She estimated that there were maybe twenty-five or thirty miles between the Myers home and her old stomping grounds.

She wished it didn't bother her so much, but there it was. She simply had to face it.

When they reached the front porch, the door opened for them. Apparently, one of the cops inside had seen them coming.

"Agents," the cop at the door said with a grim nod.

Camille could hear the sobbing of a wrecked mother coming from inside, deeper within the house.

"Have you gotten anything out of them yet?" Palmer asked.

"Not much. But I think we still have some time. Once it really hits...you know how it goes."

"I do," Camille said as they stepped inside. "Thanks, officer."

With that, they stepped into the house and followed the sound of the mother's wailing and the hushed yet angry tones of a father that had just lost his daughter.

Their footsteps on the floor were muffled by the beige carpet in the entryway. The house was small, with a simple design. The living room had old furniture and a basic TV. There were shoes scattered along the floor and an easy chair that looked worn out.

It didn't take long to find the shattered couple. They were in the small kitchen and were leaning on each other for support. The father, Eric Myers, was a thin man with graying hair, a goatee, and wire-frame glasses. His eyes were red and swollen. His wife, Susan, was a very attractive woman but the talons of grief had started tearing at her.

"And you are?" the mother asked through a voice thick with mucus and tears.

"Agents Grace and Palmer," Camille said. "Believe me, ma'am. I hate to bother parents in this situation but being that it was so recent..."

"The cops say there were more of them," the father said. "More girls, taken and k..k...and killed just like our Ellie. Is that right?"

"Yes, sir. And we—"

"How many?" he demanded.

Camille didn't see the point in pulling punches. They'd just lost their daughter. There wasn't anything she was going to tell them that would be worse than that.

"Three others. All in the last week."

The father shook his head while his wife sat in a chair at the table. Her hands gripped the edge of the table as if she feared she might float away without it.

"We have some footage for the security cameras at the Quick-Go," Palmer said. "But it looks like we won't be able to use much of it. There's just nothing to go on. For right now, we really just need to ask a few very important questions. You won't like some of them, but we have to ask."

"Go on, then," the husband said. Camille could tell he just wanted to get on with it because he wasn't going to be able to remain the strong one for much longer.

"Did Ellie ever spend much time in the French Quarter?"

"No," the mother said. "She hated the Quarter. She did the whole Mardi Gras thing last year but...that was never really her scene. She was...she's an introvert. Hates being around lots of people. Partying at bars really wasn't her thing."

"I don't think she was much of a partier," the father added.

"Mr. and Mrs. Myers," Camille said, "this is the first time the killer has struck outside of the city. It raises the question of whether Ellie was being targeted for a specific reason...if there was maybe a connection there. Can you think of any estranged boyfriends or anything like that?"

"She's only ever had one," the father said. "That ended on good terms last year when he went off to college at BYU. She's had guys sort of calling on her but I don't think...no, I don't think anyone was ever mad at her."

"What about voodoo?" Camille asked. "Was she even involved in voodoo in any way? Even just a passing interest?"

The mother seemed aghast at this, as if someone had called her a very bad name. The father, on the other hand, seemed shocked that it was even a question.

"No," the mother said vehemently.

"Or, rather, if she did, she never told us," the father said. "And she told us everything. She was very open with us."

"Was she still living here with you?" Camille asked.

"Yes. She'd been looking for an apartment. She...she..."

It was there that Camille understood they'd lost the mother. As if on cue, she got to her feet and hurried out of the room. She managed a weak and strangled "Sorry, excuse me," as she disappeared into the dark hallway beyond.

"I should go check on her," the husband said.

"Of course," Camille replied. "Would you mind if we had a look in her room?"

He grimaced at this, as if someone had stabbed him right in the heart. "I don't see why not," he whispered. "It's down the hall, first door on the left."

He headed in that same direction to follow his wife, and Camille and Palmer followed behind him. They found the door to Ellie's bedroom opened, revealing a tidy room that looked like just about every other older girl's bedroom Camille had ever seen.

There was a desk with a laptop computer, the lid closed. There were a few small bookshelves stuffed with paperbacks. Camille scanned it and found a few horror titles, a few thick graphic novels, and multiple books on the band Nirvana. But nothing at all related to voodoo or the occult.

As she checked out the books, Palmer looked under the bed and in the small closet. It took less than three minutes to figure out that there was nothing that would answer any of their questions.

When they headed back to the kitchen, they found it remained empty. They could hear the mother still weeping from further down the hallway. Camille and Palmer stood there for a moment, looking down the dark hallway. "Maybe we can come back later," Palmer suggested. "Right now, I don't see them being much help. And understandably so." He glanced to the solemn faced cop standing in the corner and said, "Let us know if they offer up anything useful, would you?"

The cop nodded as Camille and Palmer took their leave. Camille hated that a set of parents were experiencing such pain, but she was also relieved that she and Palmer had spent no more than ten minutes in the house.

The afternoon sun was casting the yard in an odd orange-tinged glow. Camille found herself looking behind the house again, to that strip of forest. Not too far behind all of that, her history was waiting for her...if she chose to revisit it.

"This asshole is starting to irritate me," Palmer said out of nowhere as they reached the car. "How the hell is he striking so quickly and leaving nothing behind?"

Camille was too stuck with her own demons to form any rational response. She did, however, find it odd that the killer had struck at a convenience store. Every convenience store had at least one camera these days. Surely, he'd known it; it was why he'd walked in with his head down, never looking in the direction of where a camera might be.

"Hey, Grace?"

She snapped out of her private thoughts, feeling a surge of irritation. "Yeah?" she said, nearly snapping.

"You good?"

"Yeah. Just like you said: it's frustrating."

They'd reached the car now and she knew he was on to her. His eyes were still on her when she looked back to the trees one last time.

"Your old home isn't too far away from here, huh?"

"Too close for comfort, that's for sure. But...how would you know?"

"I knew you were coming. I wanted to know about who I was working with. You grew up not too far from here, right? In Upping?"

"Yes. And we're not going to talk about that."

Her voice raised with each word and though she knew she was basically yelling at him, she didn't care. Sure, there was no way he could know he'd hit a sore point, but she also didn't feel like calling it out. What gave him permission to ask something like that, anyway? It's not like they were friends, getting to know one another.

"Shit. Sorry. My bad."

There was a sarcastic edge to his tone that grated on her nerves. "My past, my business," she said.

"Hey," he said, snapping right back as he cranked the car. "I got it. My mistake."

He pulled away from the Myers home with a growing tension in the car. They left there with Camille feeling defeated on two fronts. First, in still having no answers on the case and secondly because her demons were coming back to screw with her and they were still over thirty miles away.

CHAPTER TWENTY SEVEN

They parted ways at the field office and Camille didn't like that she was so relieved by it. Palmer figured he'd get quicker results with the security footage from the Quick-Go if he worked out of his own office. Camille agreed and took a bureau sedan to head back out to the French Quarter.

Only, she had no intention of going to the French Quarter. As far as she was concerned, it was no longer a location of interest for this case.

Besides, as soon as they'd left the Myers' home, she'd felt that pull...the pull to go to Upping. Even if she just drove through the piece of shit town to prove to herself that it really had no true hold on her, it would be worth the trip.

She had to lay these old skeletons and demons to rest if she was going to solve this case. She'd left Alabama thinking she'd be perfectly fine working so close to where she'd grown up, but had been proven wrong pretty swiftly.

She took the sedan back the way she and Palmer had come, only she took a left that wound even further back into the woods before reaching the secondary road the Quick-Go was located on.

The roads started to feel familiar right away. The lay of the land was a bit different; the forests were a bit thicker and the edges of the two-lane roads had been widened out a bit. She followed the road with a childlike trust, her heart torn in a million directions as she inched into her hometown of Upping.

The lay of the land in approaching the town may have changed but the town of Upping had remained very much the same. She took in the familiar sights as she passed by and felt like there was a ghost breathing down her neck.

She passed through the same empty main street and the same dumpy little shops and houses. All the same people inhabited the streets, albeit in a few different forms. There was the same convenience store, the same diner, the same bar.

It was like she'd stepped into an alternative timeline where her life had played out exactly the same as it had the first time but everything had just aged an extra fifteen years.

The familiarity of it all was sickening. Her blood boiled and her heart ached for the same reason it had a decade before.

Why are you here? she asked herself. *The demons aren't real demons. Your father is probably glad you're out of his life because you represent so much guilt and sadness. Your old home isn't here anymore. There is nothing for you here.*

But as she passed the Upping Diner, she wasn't so sure that was true. There was one place that did not automatically make her cringe when she thought of it, one person that may be of some value. One person that had always been a bright light in an otherwise dark place. She could see the little strip of dirt road in her head and felt that same pull...the need to go, the need to revisit.

She didn't even waste time with doubting it would be worth it. Nothing else in the stupid town had changed. Why would Deanna Lewiston?

She thought of Deanna as she redirected herself, cutting north to the far edge of Upping. Going this route, she passed more familiar-but-eerie sights.

The dingy strip mall with the small grocery store with hand-drawn signs in the window to promote that week's specials, the hardware store that always seemed to be selling nail guns or pressure washers or some other loud tool. The same small, mom and pop restaurants that served the same food day in, day out.

The same, redbrick houses bordering the same roads. Small glimpses of the past. They were the same, just aged, but she had a very different perspective on them now.

Camille turned the sedan down the old, dirt road she'd seen in her head. It had been such a fixture in her childhood. She knew it as well as she knew her own name. Camille pulled into the driveway, noticing a few things that had changed.

Once pristine, the house was now lacking paint. The yard was overgrown and there was a strange, abandoned car in the front yard.

Deanna Lewiston, it seemed, had not been immune to the decay of Upping, Louisiana.

When Camille had been a young girl, Deanna had been an aunt of sorts, the sort of aunt that has no real blood relation to the family. It started out as Deanna babysitting Camille and then, when Camille was ten or so, a place for Camille to retreat to when things got stressful at home.

After Nanette had gone missing, Deanna had been more of a parent than her mother and father. Deanna had kept Camille sane when the world made no sense.

She had not seen Deanna in over eight years, and they hadn't spoken for six. There had been no real reason for this, other than time, career, and the urge to keep her past as far away from her mind as possible—even the better parts of it.

So when Camille parked her car and started walking across the yard to the old, wooden porch, she felt both at home and out of place at the same time.

She knocked on the door, not sure what to hope for. Did she want Deanna to be home or out and about, petering around Upping?

She didn't get her answer until Deanna Lewiston opened the door and the past was smiling out at her. A look of disbelief slowly spread across Deanna's face as she opened the door.

Camille wasn't prepared for the surge of emotion when Deanna stepped out onto the porch without a word and embraced her.

She didn't know what to say, but she let Deanna hold her. She just stood there on the porch of her childhood home, weeping into the arms of the one positive thing Upping had given her.

Camille let Deanna hold her for a while before pulling back and sniffling.

She smiled, wiping tears from her cheek as Deanna looked on. "Long time, no see," Camille said, trying to be funny but failing.

"I'll say," Deanna replied. "My God, Camille. You're a looker now."

"I was a looker when I was ten," Camille said, feeling herself smile. "What have you been up to, D?"

"You know. The same old, same old. What about *you*? What on earth are you doing in Upping?"

"I um, I'm on a case here," Camille said, a bit unsure of herself. "Well, up in New Orleans, anyway."

Deanna's eyes were still a bit wet; she wiped at them as she laughed. "So your work brought you back home?"

"Yes, in a roundabout way."

Deanne stared at her for a moment longer and then blinked, as if in surprise. "Ah, those damned manners. Not sure where they went. Come on in, honey. My God, it's nice to see you."

Camille smiled and followed her inside. She'd expected to see the same furniture, the same carpets, the same everything. She was not disappointed. The large rug in the living room was more faded than she recalled, and the thin curtains, though still pulled to the side, were the same shade of deep navy.

But she was not expecting the absolute wash of nostalgia and safety that came over her as she stepped inside. She did, in a way, feel as if she'd walked directly into a picture from the better memories of her childhood.

She sat down on the couch and Deanna sat down beside her. "So, let me see if I can figure this out," Deanna said. "I knew you were an FBI agent. People hear things, you know. You show up on my doorstep while on a case. It makes me think you're either lost out in the woods or the case is whooping you good."

"Oh, it's whooping me REAL good." She snickered a bit, unable to take her eyes off of Deanna. The years had been good to her. She had to be reaching sixty by now but she looked no older than forty-five. Very few gray hairs, a great complexion, and the same winning Deanna smile.

"So I'm your inspiration? You wanted to come by to see the one good thing this town ever offered you?"

"Jesus, D. Maybe you should be with the FBI, too."

"Have you...well, have you been by to see your dad?"

Camille shook her head. "No. And I'm not going to. I'm not ready for that."

"I don't think anyone would blame you. Not even your father." There was an awkward silence between them, which Deanna ended with a sigh and then saying, "So...you wanna tell me about this case?"

"I can't. I just...I don't know. I stayed away from here for so long and then this case brought me so damned close to it all. Not just emotionally, but physically. It *literally* brought me to the doorstep of my past. And yes...you were the one good thing to come out of that and I had to see you. I had to remember that my entire past is not demons, mistakes and...and just this huge pile of utter shit."

"I think you're maybe being just a little too hard on yourself. Ah, but you always did have a flair for the dramatic."

"You shut your mouth," Camille said, laughing.

"So, how long can you stay?"

"Not long," Camille said. "I'm supposed to be in the French Quarter right now."

"Oh, honey, you took a *big* wrong turn. You got time for coffee?"

"Do you already have it on?"

130

"You know me. I *keep* it on."

"Then sure. One cup."

Deanna hurried away into the adjoining kitchen. Camille could hear her opening the cabinets and getting cups out. "You know, I don't think we've ever had coffee together," she called out. "How do you take it?"

"Just a bit of sugar, please."

As she waited, Camille got up and paced around the living room. It was all so familiar, but different, too. The same curtains, the same rug, the same pictures on the wall, the same books on the built-in bookcase.

She scanned the books, smiling as her eyes scanned a few familiar titles. Most of them bright smiles to her face: the collection of Emily Dickinson poems, a huge book on the different species of birds found in Louisiana swamps, the trashy romance books she often got scolded for leafing through.

But then she stopped scanning. Her heart seemed to leap in her throat and before she knew what she was doing, she was reaching for a slim volume, its spine lightly battered.

It was titled: Voodoo and the Creole Approach.

She remembered this book, but had never bothered looking at it deeply. But she had opened it up, just as she'd opened up every other book on these shelves. She recalled some of the pictures, some of the chapter titles. Now, though...now it seemed like the most important book on the shelf.

She cracked the book open and right away thought about something she'd discussed with Dr. Penderhook and Palmer. She'd mentioned it in passing, as just as comparative note. But now, so many victims later, it seemed much heavier.

And she was ashamed of herself for not thinking of it again.

She'd not liked the book as a kid because it had seemed dark in nature. It had been the first time in her childhood where she'd considered there was a very real aspect to voodoo, not just spooky lore her father told her.

She looked at the table of contents and saw a familiar name, a name she'd briefly spooked Palmer with.

"What if..." she said to the book.

Deanna suddenly appeared with two cups of coffee. She looked inquisitively at Camille and smiled.

"You look...determined."

"Good," Camille said. "Keep that in mind as I tell you that I have to go. I think...I think I just figured something out."

"So, I sort of helped?"

Camille stepped toward one of the only people she'd ever fully trusted and kissed her on the cheek. "More than you know."

"You better come see me again before you leave town."

"Try to stop me," she called out as she ran for the door.

She hopped in the sedan and cranked it, not even realizing that she'd accidentally taken Deanna's book until she was back out on the road.

CHAPTER TWENTY EIGHT

Palmer rubbed at his eyes as he leaned back in his chair, averting his eyes form the computer screen he'd been staring at for the better part of an hour. He'd been fighting the logical conclusion that he'd need to eventually get eye glasses, but moments like these wore him down. He'd been reading over case files related to voodoo, going back as much as twenty years.

The hell of it was that most reports that involved any mention of voodoo were scant at best. There was rarely any violence associated with them and those that were questioned or even arrested seemed to be mostly agreeable.

He was beginning to come to an alarming understanding. They were working on a case that seemed to lean heavily toward voodoo or some other sort of ritualistic practice, but there just wasn't enough evidence or historical reports in the area to study.

He supposed it was just about time to redirect his search—to start looking for cases outside of the voodoo realm and narrow it down to the bodies of nude women found in the woods. But he knew that would open up entire case files of murders and could easily waste valuable time.

Currently, he was sitting in a small, temporary office at a New Orleans precinct. If he couldn't find what he needed here about local crimes, he also had bureau resources. And God only knew how deep that well of cases would go.

With no other real choice, he leaned forward in his chair again to start the search. As he started typing in his filter terms, the door to his small, borrowed office opened. He looked over his shoulder and was surprised to see Camille.

"I figured you might have taken a bit longer in the Quarter," he said. He wasn't sure how to speak to her. He was still a little offset by her reaction from earlier when he'd asked questions about her history with the area.

"I'm going to be honest," she said as she came into the room. "I didn't go the Quarter. I had...well, I had some things I needed to get done. Some places I needed to go."

"Upping?"

She nodded and Palmer could sense some tension there. "And you can berate me about that later. For now, though, I think I might have something of breakthrough. And you're going to have to hold off all judgment and hear me out."

He repositioned his chair so he could look directly at her. Folding his arms, he said, "Okay. Try me."

"We've been assuming this has been voodoo related. And it's been weird because, let's face it, who wants to be the agent that gets mired down in a case about voodoo? A practice that a lot of people outside of this area scoff at as being silly superstition?"

"I follow you so far." This HAD been a chief concern of his. It had ever since he'd first come to the area and heard whispers of secret voodoo circles and even a few respected practitioners.

"But what if this is something beyond simple voodoo? What if this is some sort of black magic?"

"Well, for one...voodoo is real. Magic is not."

"On its face, you're right. But what if the markings on the bodies, the little bumps all along the chests, are part of some arcane, obscure ritual? Sure, magic may not be real, but the history of people practicing black magic is *very* real."

"So you think the killer might be in the middle of some sort of dark magic, occult-style work?"

"I think it's worth looking into. I have to admit that I do keep forgetting just how deep those roots are in some communities around here."

"Now, by black magic," Palmer said, "just so I'm clear...we're talking about so-called supernatural magic that is used for selfish gain, right? Actual spells, hexes, and things like that?"

"Yes," Camille said, clearly a bit uncomfortable with the idea.

Palmer leaned back in the chair again and thought this over. "Earlier, you mentioned that Serpent and the Rainbow book. Is that the sort of stuff you're talking about?"

"Could be. But without knowing what sort of drugs they're being injected with, I have no idea. Outside of that book and a few spooky stories I heard growing up, it's just not an area I'm super knowledgeable in."

Palmer chuckled a bit. "Well, it just so happens, I've been looking over voodoo related files. And while the terms 'back magic' and 'occult' tend to be avoided, there IS a name that kept popping up. Never as a suspect but as someone to question. Even someone used as a consultant from time to time."

"Got an address?"

Palmer sighed and turned back to the laptop that had been wearing his eyes out. "As it turns out, I do."

***

While Palmer had never put much stock into voodoo folklore, he was still unnerved and a little creeped out whenever he was in the presence of voodoo artifacts. He was reminded of this uneasiness when, half an hour later, he and Camille stepped into a shop called Old Man Hex's.

It was owned by a man named Moses Saintil, a staple of the voodoo community in New Orleans for the better part of two decades. The shop itself was small but felt much more authentic that the numerous novelty voodoo shops in the area.

When he stepped inside, Palmer took a moment to orient himself wanting to make sure he did not close his mind off to whatever conversations they may have with Moses.

"You ever been in one of these places before?" he asked Camille.

"A few times in my teens. All touristy-type shops though. This one, though...it feels like the real deal."

This was true, and Palmer felt it everywhere he looked.

On the right-side wall, there was an impressive collection of authentic voodoo art and artifacts. One corner of the shop was dedicated to a large selection of gris-gris bags and other items one could wear or carry to ward off evil spirits or bring good luck. A particularly large collection of lucky hand talismans filled a whole wall. Some of them looked like they were over a hundred years old. To the left and just straight ahead, there were shelves filled with voodoo dolls and fetish objects, as well as paintings that undoubtedly depicted voodoo spirits and gods.

The air was thick with the smell of incense, and Palmer was willing to bet that it was all done in the traditional manner.

Beyond all of the stock, there was a small counter in the corner that shielded the proprietor from view. He was an older back man, his long beard having gone totally gray. He regarded them with eyes that looked almost completely bloodshot.

"You two interested in some protection?" the proprietor asked.

135

"Protection from what?"

The man shrugged his thin, brittle shoulders.

"You look like cops. Maybe detectives? And you look troubled. So I figure maybe you're here for protections."

He had a thick accent that bordered on French, making Palmer assume he was of Haitian decent.

"Are you Moses Saintil?" Palmer asked.

"Yes, that's me."

"You were partially, right," Camille, said, stepping forward to show her badge. "We're agents Grace and Palmer, with the FBI. We were hoping you could help us with a case we are working on."

Moses seemed chagrinned over this. He wasn't necessarily irritated, but there was an air of offense to him. "Do you know for sure it is voodoo related?"

"We are quite sure."

"Good. Because I have had far too many people accuse voodoo of crimes they do not understand. Dark and messed up crimes? Must be voodoo!" He barked a dry laughter at them, shaking his head. "What is this crime?"

"Four dead women," Palmer said. "All injected with something unidentifiable right along their hip. There are little pock marks between their breasts, almost like bug bites."

"I see. And where were the bodies found?"

"All were found in the forest," Camille said. "They were positioned on stumps and logs, as if they were being displayed."

Moses thought about this for a moment and Palmer saw some of the contempt slide off of him. He seemed interested now...maybe even concerned.

"That would be something dark. Dark magic, perhaps."

Palmer bristled at the comment. "What do you mean? What sort of rituals are involved?"

"Things that sound much like this. What you are describing is not standard voodoo. Most voodoo has been given terrible rumors and stereotypes. It is mostly used as a form of blessing, healing, and good fortunes. But black magic...that is something different. It had its evil roots n voodoo, yes, but..."

"Sir, what can you tell us about black magic?" Grace asked. "Nothing based on stories or folklore. What is something realistic that we can pursue?"

Moses seemed to really give this some thought. It wasn't a figure of speech or a joke or a storyteller's yarn; it was something real to him...something he considered to be a real and terrible danger.

"Many people pretend to know much, but few do. The first thing to know is that black magic is a very rare thing. It is something that is only practiced by those who had at least one parent or grandparent who knew it. It isn't something that is learned from a book, although some do try that. And not all the things in books work, let me tell you."

He paused here and eyed them carefully, as if making sure they really wanted to keep going. When neither stopped him, Moses continued.

"There are two forms of black magic. One is the more powerful, but the less common. This one requires the sacrifice of a human. It is only possible to perform it if the intended victim is alive when it is done."

"And the other?" Camille asked.

"This one is more common, but is not exactly magic. It is more ritualistic. Like what you are saying. And the reason I think these murders fall into this category rather than the first is that they were injected. You're certain of this?"

"Yes," Camille said. "All four, in the same place."

"And this ritualistic one," Palmer said, "what type of ritual is it?"

"If these victims are being injected and killed afterwards, I believe you want to look into the zombi."

"The *what*?" Palmer said.

"Not like you're thinking," Camille said. "It's like what I told you about before...the rituals out in Haiti."

"Zombi?" Palmer said, incredulous.

"Yes," Moses said. "It is indeed a Haitian concept. There were literal means to create a sort of *half* human. A zombie...a reanimated corpse with only half a soul."

"But these victims are *dead*," Palmer said. "Not reanimated."

"Perhaps that means the practitioner is not very good. Perhaps he is practicing until he can get it right."

Camille took the lead while Palmer tried to digest all. She stepped closer to the counter and softened her voice.

"Do you know anyone that practices black magic like this?"

"Not anymore. I distanced myself from those people. But I *can* tell you where you can start looking."

"Good," Camille said. "That would be fantastic. Where is it?"

Once again, Moses sized them up. "I will tell you," he said. "But first, I really think you should re-consider my offer for protections."

A chill rode up Palmer's spine that made him realize he was willing to try just about anything. Not just to get the hell out of this man's store but because this case seemed to have just taken a significantly darker turn.

CHAPTER TWENTY NINE

Even having grown up near the area and hearing about voodoo and some spooky stories that revolved around it, Camille could not push her mind away from the stereotype that any community based around some of the more sinister corners of voodoo would be in backwoods hollers. She *knew* it to not be necessarily true, but that's where her mind went.

However, the location Moses gave them was an apartment building in a poor part of town. It was far removed from the French Quarter, a shadow of the city that the lights and excitement of Mardi Gras and a partying atmosphere did not touch. Located just about a mile west of an area known the Seventh Ward, it was an area that still seemed to live in the wake of Hurricane Katrina, not yet able to really reclaim its footing.

The apartment building sat beside an abandoned parking lot and yet another apartment building. Pulling up in front of them as the afternoon rolled on, Camille could easily imagine the danger of the place at night.

According to Moses, this was a building where he often sent many medicinal herbs and unfiltered salts, as they came to him through online orders. The salts, he'd stated, were often used in some dark magic rituals. Not only that, but the building itself was rumored to be the home of a secretive bokor—the voodoo equivalent of a sorcerer.

Having no apartment number or physical address, they had nowhere to start looking. For a moment, Camille felt like she was simply on a beat, hoping to run into someone that might be able to help them.

As it turned out, it didn't take that long. She was quite certain unemployment numbers were pretty high in the outer regions of the city, so there were several people simply loitering about as they got out of the car and started looking around the block.

The first person they approached was a woman that looked to be in her early twenties. She was wearing a hooded sweatshirt that was far too big for her and reeked of marijuana smoke. When she saw the two agents approaching her, she seemed freaked out for a moment but then resumed her position against the wall of a small convenience store.

"You live around here?" Camille asked the woman.

"Who's asking?"

"FBI." Camille showed her badge, doing so quickly and trying not to make a big production out of it.

"Shit," the woman said. "I...hey, look, I..."

"You've done nothing wrong," Camille assured her. "We're just looking for someone that we believe lives in this area."

"Who?"

"We don't have a name. But we think it's going to be someone involved in voodoo. Maybe someone that doesn't come out much. Maybe someone you've heard stories about. Anything like that around here that you can think of?"

After a few seconds of silence, the woman nodded and pointed down the street. "There's a building there. I don't know if I should say it..."

Camille followed the woman's finger and saw that she was pointing to the very same building they'd parked in front of. The same building Moses had directed them to.

"Why not say it?" Palmer asked.

"Man, that shit is evil. I mean, I respect it and all, but I *have* heard some stories. But I stay out of there."

"Do you know him? Have you seen him? It's a man?"

"Yeah, it's a dude. I've seen him a few times. I don't even know if he actually lives there."

"You know his name by any chance?"

"Not a real name, nah. I think they call him Mizer."

"The few times you've seen him, have you seen anyone with him?"

"Yeah shady types. Looked like drug addicts...all frail and sort of just shuffling around, you know?"

"If we could—" Camille started, but her concentration was broken by the sound of approaching footsteps.

She turned and saw an elderly African American woman walking toward them. The woman had to be close to eighty, her face thin and wrinkled, her eyes narrowed behind a pair of glasses that looked as if they hadn't been cleaned in ages. She walked with a walking stick which she suddenly lifted up and pointed at the girl.

"You get yo'self outta here, Charlene!"

"But, Mama, they was just asking me—"

"And I give a damn why? I said git!"

The girl looked hurt but did as the old woman said. The girl—Charlene, apparently—lowered her head and started walking away

140

quickly in the opposite direction. She glanced back over her shoulder only a single time, looking like a sad, scolded dog.

"Ma'am," Palmer said, "We were in the middle of asking her questions. We're FBI agents, looking for someone we believe lives in that building over there, and she could have helped."

"Yeah, I know. I heard you when I came 'round the corner. But you don't need to be botherin' that poor girl with this madness."

"She called you Ma," Camille said. "Are you related?"

"Hello no. You see that girl? Just as white as snow. Dirty snow but snow all the same. Most of the kids 'round here call me Ma."

"So you know the area well?"

"I do. And I know that man you're looking for. But you may as well go on back to where you came. Ain't nothing to find with that man but darkness."

"You mean the man the girl said some call Mizer?"

"That's the one."

"What do you know about him?" Palmer asked.

The woman tapped her walking stick rather nervously on the ground and shook her head. "Too damn much."

"Ma'am, we need to speak to him about several murders in the area. It's important we speak to him. If there is anything at all you could tell us, it would be a huge help."

When the old woman sighed, her entire frame seemed to shake. "I can tell you what I know, and it ain't much. Just that he's...well, he's dark."

"Anything at all would be helpful," Palmer said.

"The man, Mizer, he lives in that building right there. But you shouldn't go there. The people who live 'round him, they stay outside. They ain't meant to be talking to him, you know?"

"You mean they fear him," Camille said.

"They fear what he is. He's not right. You feel the darkness coming off of him."

"What do you mean?"

"I mean, he ain't like you and me. He's got powers. All sorts of it. He looks at you, and you do whatever he wants you to. You don't have a choice."

"He controls people?" Palmer asked.

"I suppose that's what it is."

"Do you also live in that building, ma'am?"

"No. I have a house two blocks over."

"So then how have you seen him?" Camille asked

"Because it ain't the only place he lives." The old woman eyed them with skepticism. "He done something bad?"

"We don't know. But we think he can at least help us on a case. Young girls are dying, ma'am. If there's anything at all—"

"He's got a house, too. A bit down the road from my own. I don't think he actually owns it. One of the little shits he hangs out with does. Just looking at the place will make you go cold. I think he just practices his magic there."

"Could you show us where it is?" Camille asked.

"I don't know," the old woman said, still tapping at the cracked sidewalk with her walking stick. "You buy into it?"

"Into what?" Palmer asked.

"That black magic voodoo."

"Right now we're just trying to find a killer," Palmer said.

"You dodged the question, son. But let me tell you: whether or not you hold stock in it, it can get into you. I seen it around here with these kids. It's appealing to them. Something risky, something different Something they know would scare their parents. It's an evil world, agents. And sometimes the devil is right next door."

She looked back behind her, in the direction of an empty four-way intersection. Again, she sighed and this time she nodded to them.

"Come on then," she said. "Come on and I'll show you."

"Actually," Camille said, "we have our car just right over there. Let us give you a ride home."

"Sounds polite of you," she said. "Thank you kindly."

With that, they walked the old woman to their sedan. She didn't say anything else, and Camille was perfectly fine with that. The chill that refused to leave her bones was convinced the woman had said enough.

CHAPTER THIRTY

Camille helped the old woman out of the car and walked her to her front door. The house was in need of repairs. It was a simple one-story box a place with a crooked cement block for a front porch. An old car sat in the driveway, the left tire removed and sitting on a block.

The old woman looked out across the street and nodded down the block. "It's right down there," she said. "End of the block, take a right and it's the first house you'll come to."

"Thank you."

"Don't thank me, child," the woman said. "This Mizer character is no good. FBI or not, I don't like it."

Camille hated that she was so spooked by the woman's words but she couldn't deny it. Rather than say anything, Camille simply gave the woman a polite nod and headed back to the still-running car.

Palmer backed out and headed to the end of the block. He took the right as Camille pointed it out and slowly pulled over to the side of the street. He did not park directly in front of the house, but closer to the neighboring house.

Both houses looked very much the same as the one the old woman lived in. When they got out of the car, it was 4:10 in the afternoon and the entire neighborhood seemed deathly quiet.

Camille and Palmer walked across the yard and up onto the porch. Palmer knocked on the peeling wooden door as casually as he could. Right away, they could hear something moving inside Muffled feet moved around and old boards creaked. Camille thought she could hear light whispering but wasn't certain.

"Well, someone's home," Palmer said. "But they clearly don't want visitors."

They waited another twenty seconds, but there was no answer. Camille looked back to the old woman's house, wondering if she might be watching them from a window. She hoped not. Already, as they waited at the door, she felt the old woman had been right. Something about this house felt off...felt *dark*.

Camille knocked next, a little harder. She listened for movement inside, but there was nothing.

"Should we allow ourselves in?" Palmer asked.

"We don't have just cause," Camille said, hating that it was her first response.

"Maybe we can find something," he said. "Maybe around back?"

It was a decent idea, and Camille was already tired of waiting. Especially when she knew there was someone inside. Quickly and quietly, she stepped off of the porch and made her way around the small, decrepit house.

Camille went to the front of the house and peeked to the right. There was a large, overgrown side yard, borne up by only an old and rusted water hose holder that had popped off of the side of the house. Further along, there was an old clothesline and nothing more.

She hurried along the side yard and came to the back. The backyard looked a lot like the front yard, overgrown and with a distinct sense of abandonment. As she walked around the house, Camille could hear the sound of Palmer trying the front door again.

The back door looked just as beaten up as the front. A single window looked out onto the backyard and for just a moment, Camille thought she saw movement in it. Her instincts had her hand go to her sidearm. She allowed herself to pull it, knowing it might be a bit premature but feeling safer for having done it.

From the backyard, she could also see that the house had a basement. The very top rim of the concrete frame poked out from the dirt and weeds before the mildew-stained vinyl siding took over. A short, rectangular window sat low to the ground, dingy with dirt and grime.

She started heading for it to see if she could get a peek inside. She'd taken two steps when she heard a muffled cry.

A scared cry. A woman's moan.

That was all she needed to hear. She quick retraced her steps around the sideboard, moving as silently as she could. She didn't even wait to get back on the porch with Palmer before she said, "Cries of distress inside. Coming from a basement."

"No more knocking?" he asked, already taking a big step back.

"No more knocking," she agreed.

Camille fell in behind Palmer as he rushed forward with a huge kick. The door swung off its hinges, clattering to the floor.

Camille felt even more secure when she saw just how easily she and Palmer managed to fall into flanking positions. She sensed that he was covering them fully on the left, so she took the right.

144

The interior of the house didn't offer much. The front door opened up onto a hallway. That hall led directly into a kitchen just ahead of them. To the right, there was a small living area. She noted that there were two chairs, a small coffee table, and no television. The coffee table was littered with an ashtray, two incense burners, and several books. Though she did not closely study the left, as Palmer had it covered, she caught enough details to note that they passed by a single bedroom and a small bathroom.

When they entered the kitchen, the smell of garbage greeted them. Old pizza boxes and a few Chinese takeout containers were on the table and by the door beside an overflowing trashcan.

From the back of the kitchen, the door to the backyard sat in the wall. To the right, tucked between a small refrigerator and the start of a small kitchen counter, a thin door stood. It was slightly ajar, revealing a thin sliver of darkness.

"Basement," Camille mouthed.

And with that, she stepped forward. Her right hand held her Glock, her left hand falling on the doorknob. She pulled the door open slowly, revealing darkness and the top of a set of old, wooden stairs leading down.

In between moves, Palmer looked at her for a second of eye contact, two fingers pressing against his lips. She nodded and stepped forward. As she place her first foot down into the darkness, the smell hit her right away.

Pungent sweat. Human excrement. Vomit.

She stepped as silently as she could, but the stairs still creaked under her weight. She didn't really mind, as she figured the front door crashing in had given them away. She listened for further sounds of the moaning, crying woman but heard nothing. There were only her footfalls, her breath, her heartbeat in her ears.

She felt Palmer behind her, his presence in the darkness feeling almost like a shield. The basement below was dark, lit up only by the light from the kitchen behind them and the small window she'd seen out in the backyard. Still, she made it down fine, her eyes having adjusted just enough.

She pivoted off of the stairs and swiveled herself around in a one-hundred-and-eighty-degree arc, ready to open fire if it came down to it.

But the basement was empty.

Jesus, she thought. *Did I not* really *hear anything from outside? Did I just imagine it?*

But that thought came to a crashing halt as she stepped further away from the stairs and got a good look at the basement.

Ahead of her and slightly to the right was what appeared to be a small worktable. Beside it was another table, this one with a darker hue and oddly rounded shapes. There were cut marks all along it and a variety of stains that were visible even in the poor light of the basement.

It was a butcher's block.

While the block itself was empty, the worktable revealed quite a bit. It was pretty much like looking at the shelves of any voodoo shop...and, in some cases, peeking into the nightmare of a deranged person.

The table was littered with all sorts of voodoo items and other oddities.

Glass jars lay on their sides, some filled with a black liquid. Others were filled with an odd-colored powder or grain of some kind. There were all sorts of bizarre plant snippets—petals, roots, bulbs of all kind. There were feathers and small figurines, some of which were carved with intricate designs and painted with various colors.

Located to the right side of the table, stored in a piece of plastic Tupperware, there were a series of bones. They were small, and she thought they likely belonged to a chicken.

Palmer stepped in beside her and pointed to something laying on the floor, nearly hidden in the shadows.

It was a dead frog. It was lying on its back, its white underbelly exposed. It had been cut open and peeled back, its insides stripped out.

And then, just a few feet beyond that, she saw a door.

It was wooden and looked old enough to have come out of a castle in some strange medieval tale. The door was copper and there was an old-style lock plate on the outside.

Camille and Palmer approached it, guns drawn. Camille looked to Palmer and gave a little nod.

Palmer took a breath and took a shooter's stance. Then, keeping his voice as calm as possible, he said: "Come out, Mizer. This is Agent Palmer with the FBI. I know you're in there. I heard movement. And we also know there's a woman in there. You come out of your own accord, or I'll come in myself."

They waited a few seconds and though there was no initial response, they DID hear movement. It was nothing more than a faint, scuffling footstep, but it was enough.

The soft shuddering gasp that followed made it clear that they had to act.

Palmer nodded to Camille. She stepped forward, grabbed the doorknob, and pulled it open quickly. She knelt down behind it as Palmer aimed his Glock directly into the small, confined space. The air that came out was staggering. It became clear right away where the smell of excrement and puke had been coming from. It suddenly came out to fill the rest of the basement in waves.

Immediately, a man came rushing out. He moved quickly, taking advantage of the absolute darkness inside. He attacked first by slamming his shoulder into the already opened door. It collided hard with Camille and sent her to the ground. Her back smacked the concrete wall behind her, sending a flare of pain shooting through her body.

The man then went low on Palmer. He rammed his shoulders into Palmer's knees and as soon as Palmer went down, Camille saw the knife in the man's hand.

It was an old butcher knife, the blade dully glinting in the low light. The man held it high with both hands and he brought it down hard.

Camille got to her feet, gasping for the breath that went rushing out of her when she'd hit the wall. She knew she wasn't going to make it, that the blade was going to go right into Palmer's chest, but she had to at least *move*...she had to try.

Palmer was a bit quicker than the attacker, though. he brought his right hand up, still holding the Glock, and punched the man hard in the chin.

The sound was like wood being split open. The man went limp for a moment and then fell to the side. The knife dropped to the floor and Palmer backed away quickly.

Camille redirected her attack and pounced on the fallen man. As she did so, she got her first good look at him. He appeared to be rather tall—maybe around six-three or so—and had long hair that had been gathered up into tacky dreadlocks in a few places. He had a dark complexion, but didn't appear to be African American from what she could tell. The lower half of his face was covered in blood from the punch Palmer had just delivered.

She quickly pulled the man's hands behind his back as Palmer joined her with his handcuffs already out.

"Are you the man they call Mizer?" Camille asked.

He spouted something off to them in French or, rather, a strange bastardization of French. And then he laughed. It seemed to fill the entire basement, rattling in their heads.

"To hell with him," Camille said. "Hold him right there. I want to check the—"

She'd meant to say "the room." But she didn't need to.

As they both looked that way, an emaciated figure stumbled forward. For a moment, Camille thought she was looking at a ghost. The figure that appeared before them was so thin and emaciated that she looked downright ghoulish.

She opened her mouth to say something but fell to her knees. Then, with a shuddering cry of triumph, she fell to the ground and passed out.

CHAPTER THIRTY ONE

Four were dead.

He'd killed four of them and the ritual had not worked.

On top of that, he knew he'd been sloppy with the last one. That convenience store had cameras and though he'd been very careful, he knew he'd been careless, too.

The fourth one had not been planned. He would have eventually taken a fourth one, but that had been a desperate act. He'd been by the Quick-Go before and knew when that certain girl worked. He knew her shifts, her coming and her going. She was a good match for the ritual.

But it had not worked.

He was angry and frustrated, but he knew he had to remain calm.

He would try again. Just one more time. One more girl. And if it didn't work after that, he would give up for now.

He thought of this while sitting in the French Quarter, drinking a beer at a pub while looking out of the window. He watched the pedestrians go by, many of whom had just gotten off of work and were on their way home.

He'd felt, deep down, that it had to happen in New Orleans. If the ritual was going to work, he needed to conduct it somewhere he knew well. Not just New Orleans, but in those sacred woods around the city.

Apparently, he'd been wrong.

And he also knew he'd been wrong in moving it away from the city. He'd known it the moment the fourth woman had died. She'd slipped away so quickly, as if the spirits had been displeased with him, snuffing her life out before he even had time to hope.

It had to go a certain way. And though the man everyone knew as Mizer had given him very specific instructions, it had not worked. Had the bastard neglected to tell him something? Had the death he was trying to erase not seemed important enough to him?

What the hell was he missing?

He could try again in some other place if it came down to that but everything inside of him and in the very atmosphere of New Orleans itself told him that it was supposed to happen here.

This was, after all, where his daughter had died.

149

And if he was trying to resurrect her, it had to be in the place where she had died.

He took a very big gulp of his beer as he ruminated on that.

New Orleans...the place where she died.

What if the ritual was supposed to take place in the *exact location* where she'd died?

How had he never thought of that? He'd been so invested in the dark powers Mizer said the forests were supposed to have that he'd overlooked the obvious.

A slow-blooming excitement started to form in his stomach. He nearly got up right there and then, wanting to see if this hunch was correct.

But first he had to find the woman. The sacrifice. And he needed to plan it better than he did with the fourth woman.

But two in one day? Could he do that? Would nature turn against him if he took so much life?

He didn't know, and he didn't care.

He needed Elisa back. She'd been taken unjustly, and the spirits owed him. Mizer had said that if he took certain steps, he could get her back. It would take hard work and sacrifice, but she could come back. Things might be different, but he would essentially have his daughter returned.

Elisa had been dead for six months now. She'd died in a car accident and although he knew every excruciating detail, he tried not to recall them.

Still, they sprang up in his mind every day, especially when he settled his head down on the pillow to go to sleep.

According to the police report, the accident had not been her fault.

A truck had run through a rural stop-sign, one of those large trucks that are used a lot on construction sites. Pickup truck but the larger-bodied ones. It had come barreling across the intersection and swerved into the driver's side of Elisa's car, hitting it at angle.

The car had crumpled and somehow, Elisa's left arm had been torn from her body and thrown from the car.

Nobody had stopped to help. Nobody had even seen it happen.

He'd found her at the side of the road after she'd called him on the phone. She'd barely been able to speak and even through the phone, he could hear the blood in her throat and lungs. He'd nursed her while waiting for the ambulance, but there was nothing he could do.

Her neck had been broken and her lungs were filled with blood.

She'd died in his arms, her eyes staring up at him.

And though the driver of the truck had died, too, he still felt that the world had wronged him.

Mizer had agreed. The injustice of it all was why the rituals would be working.

But now he knew what he'd been doing wrong. He needed to go back to that intersection. That's where he needed to rest the body. Right there in the road where Elise's car had been when she'd been struck. It was just twenty miles outside of the city. He'd driven by it countless times since his daughter had been buried.

He finished his beer, pulling the image of that intersection up in his head.

He had to get it right.

He got up and left the bar and paid his tab. He moved like a ghost as he got back out onto the street, his feet not feeling like his own.

It was dusk. He wanted to get back to his hotel room and start his search before true night fell.

A very big part of him wanted to drive to the site of the accident right then and there, but he knew he needed to think things through. He needed time and he wasn't sure that would happen if he saw the area. It was going to be dark soon, and he needed to be prepared.

So he walked the streets. That's where all the woman that fit the bill were, anyway.

They had to be in their early twenties, like his Elisa.

They had to be of Creole descent, like his Elisa.

Those were the only preconditions Mizer had given him. Really, all of that was only symbolic, anyway. What mattered was the ritual and his dedication to it.

He walked the streets as night started to filter in. The street lights glowed, neon in bar windows buzzed, and the city came to life.

And somewhere in the midst of it all was the human vessel that would allow his Elise back into this world.

He walked and he looked, on the hunt. He felt hopeful and surprisingly at ease as he studied the younger women he passed by.

Really, a lot of them looked remarkably similar. He had to be very cautious about who he chose. No one too sexy, no one too introverted and hiding within themselves. No one with hoodies or visible tattoos.

He walked for the better part of half an hour, walking the same three blocks once and then moving on to another section of the city and night grew thicker around him.

And then he found her.

He spied her from across the street, coming out of an upscale store selling purses and wallets. There was a bag in her hand; apparently, she'd just made a purchase.

As he came to the edge of a crosswalk, he stopped dead in his tracks. He simply watched her for a moment.

Her hair was long, just like his daughter's had been. It was pulled back in a ponytail and it swayed as she walked.

She wore sneakers, just like the ones his daughter had on that day. The high top, canvass Converse that everyone called Chuck Taylors.

She had the same skin tone as his daughter.

She was the right age.

He watched her as she walked, deep in thought.

She's the one, he thought. She would either bring Elise back or she'd be the final attempt while he was still lurking about New Orleans.

Oh, but it's going to work this time, he told himself. And already, he again saw that intersection, buried alongside the swamps twenty miles outside of the city.

He hurried his pace and watched as the girl stopped in front of a pawn shop. This allowed him to catch up with her and when she started moving again, he was only ten feet away from her, hidden by other people on the street.

He managed to get even closer and when she took out her phone, he could hear her talking on it.

"Yes, Mom...I know. Yeah, I'll be there in like an hour. Tell Dad to hold on already. Yes...I know."

Good. She had somewhere to go. Which meant she was either headed to a parking lot, parking garage, or going to grab public transit.

Ah, but if she called an Uber or hailed a taxi, then what?

Well, he couldn't let that happen.

He hurried his pace even more and reached into the inner pocket of his thin jacket. The syringe was there, waiting. He'd have to improvise with a knife, but that wasn't going to slow him down. He had one in his car, under the seat, still stained with the blood from the girl earlier in the day.

The girl moved on ahead of him and he followed.

Then, as if even nature itself was rooting for him, the girl turned right, down a side street. The street was still well-lit and heavily populated, but there was a parking garage half a block down. He knew it well; he'd even sat there for hours a few weeks ago, looking for girls that fit Elise's description.

Moments later, he watched the girl pull a set of keys from her pocket.

He smiled nervously as she walked into the parking garage. Not wanting to seem too obvious to anyone that might see him, he waited a beat and then he also entered the garage.

Her shape was shrouded in shadow ahead of him as she made her way over to the elevator along the bottom floor.

Bingo.

"Ma'am, hold the elevator please!"

He ran forward, putting on his best innocent and gangly act. She smiled at him and held her hand out to keep the doors from sliding closed.

He slipped in with her and panted, maybe a little too dramatically.

"Thanks," he said.

She only smiled and nodded.

He smiled right back as he reached into his inner pocket and grabbed the syringe.

CHAPTER THIRTY TWO

Camille was only vaguely aware of the flutter of activity outside the interrogation room door. She and Palmer had attracted a lot of attention when they'd come in with Mizer. First of all, he'd been chanting and uttering, slinging strings of curses and hexes at anyone that so much as looked at him.

And he'd done it all with a thick ribbon of saliva and blood pouring from his mouth. Palmer's punch had not only busted open Mizer's lip, but it had apparently knocked two teeth out as well.

Secondly, there was a huge rush to get updates on the woman that had been discovered in his basement. So far, Camille had heard nothing, though the medics that had arrived with the ambulance didn't seem to have high hopes.

Now, behind the closed door of the interrogation room, Mizer had calmed down a bit. He still muttered under his breath, watching the agents with wide, angry eyes. There was no fear at all in those eyes, though. All Camille saw there was malice and anger.

"How many girls have you had down there?" Palmer asked.

Mizer shook his head. He stuck his tongue out and licked the blood from his chin.

"Where'd you find her?" Palmer asked, trying again to get the man to talk.

Camille wasn't as patient. She walked directly to the table and placed her palms on it, leaning in toward Mizer. He was cuffed to the table so she was safe, but she almost *wished* he would somehow take a swing at her.

"I know you have friends and allies here in the city, people that are deep into voodoo. But when we pitch your ass into prison, no one is going to fear or revere you. You'll just be another piece of meat. A *new* piece of meat. And the crazier they think you are, the harder they'll be on you. But if you'll answer these questions for us, *maybe* it will look good when we book you."

She still saw no fear in his eyes. It made her quite sure that the only way they would get him to talk was to make them think they were shocked by what he had done. He wanted to see awe and disgust. Maybe then he would start talking.

"The girl we found in your hideaway is currently in the hospital," she said. "She's going to tell us her side of the story when she is able. What are some of the things we're going to hear, Mizer?"

He glanced at her, surprised to hear his name coming out of her mouth.

"I broke her soul," he said. "She belongs to me. She'll say nothing."

"Do you think she'll miss you when you're in prison, dodging men in the shower?"

"Mock me all you want. I've done my work. I am protected."

"I'm not mocking. I grew up around here. I know the weight of the things you do. Many people fear it and respect it. I'm just trying to make sense of it. Were you going to take her out to the woods, too?"

And there it was. An expression flickering behind his eyes that was not maniacal energy and anger.

"There were no forests. She saw only that room."

Camille stored that nugget away, acting as if it was of no real importance. She moved swiftly on, hoping it would fool Mizer while also clueing Palmer in to what she was attempting to do.

"How many were there?" she asked Mizer. "How many girls saw that room?"

"She was the first."

"Bullshit."

"No, she truly was. I was careful in my selection process. I looked for her for over a year."

"Who was she?" Palmer asked.

"No one of real importance. Just a vessel."

"What do you mean by *vessel*?" Camille asked.

"A vessel that would help me usher in a new world, one where the voodoo of my people would be respected. Many of the spells and mysteries and rites, were lost in the wake of Christianity. I have tried to reclaim them. Much of it was not meant to be forgotten."

"How long was she down there?" Camille asked, trying to dance around the absurdity of his answer.

"Two weeks."

"Christ," Palmer muttered.

"And where did you find her?" Camille asked.

"Does it matter?" Mizer said. "I am no fool. You are questioning me about a crime, yes? But I can see by your eyes and the way you waltz around your questions that it is a different crime."

"Answer her question," Palmer said. He was growing agitated, getting red in the face. "Where did you find her?"

"Savannah."

"As in Savannah, Georgia?" Camille asked.

"Yes. As I said, I hunted long and wide for her. And now the baby I have planted inside of her will grow to be my servant as well."

The air went out of the room at that comment. Camille wisely stepped away from the table, worried she might reach out and strike him at any moment. She was starting to feel sick.

"Your servant?" Palmer asked. "Servant? Is that what you were doing with the girl?" He glanced to Camille, his jaw clenching. "You were trying to make her your servant?"

"A zombi?" Camille asked.

Mizer only shrugged. "Call it what you want."

"I will," Palmer said "I'll start by calling it kidnapping and rape. I'd call it about twenty years in prison, asshole."

Camille still felt the rage swelling inside of her, but she also felt a nagging doubt at the back corners of her mind. This creep wasn't even trying to work his way out of it. He seemed almost proud of what he'd done.

She thought of his brief look of confusion when she'd mentioned the woods and locked on to it.

Before she could react in any way, there was a knock on the door. She opened it only partway and saw an officer standing there. He held two sheets of paper out to her with a nervous expression on his face.

"This is what we have on the girl that was rescued from the house."

Camille took it quickly, nodded her thanks, and closed the door again.

She looked at the first page, complete with a scanned copy of the girl's driver's license. Her address was indeed listed as Savannah, Georgia. She was a pretty brunette, the sort that would turn heads at the beach and was likely the focal point of all male eyes at any party.

Her name was Karen Henreid. Brown hair. Brown eyes. In other words, not a clear match for the four women they'd found in the woods. And it didn't take a genius to tell that she wasn't Creole; or, if she was, it was so deeply buried in her genetics that it wasn't anything to even notice.

It seemed the only thing this woman had in common with their four victims was her age.

She headed for the door, the feeling of doubt growing even stronger. "Agent Palmer, can I see you in the hall?"

Without waiting for a response, she opened the door and exited the room. Palmer followed her out quickly and she could tell that he was relieved to get a break from Mizer. She was quite sure Palmer had been ready to punch the man again.

She handed the papers over to Palmer and studied him as he looked them over.

"What do you see?"

"A girl that's lucky to be alive. And likely one that's pregnant, too, if that scumbag is to be believed. Why? What *should* I be seeing?"

"She's from Savannah, not around here. She's brunette and brown eyed, not blonde. And she doesn't look a bit Creole to me."

"Shit."

The disappointment and total loss on his face told her that he'd just figured it out, too. "None of it matches up," he said. "Not a single one of our victims was touched sexually."

"Right."

"So we caught a creep, for sure," Palmer said. "Just not *our* creep. I know it's a win, but it's not the win I wanted."

"But you know," Camille said. "This whole zombi thing popping up, and the idea of attempting resurrection through black magic, has me wondering..."

"Wondering what, exactly?"

"Try to stick with me here. But the woman in Mizer's basement...she looked sort of like a zombie, right? And zombies, at least in the Hollywood sense, are dead people that come back to life, right? So what if our killer is thinking along those lines?"

"Clear it up a bit more," Palmer said with excited eyes.

"Maybe we need to start looking at cases where women are already dead. Maybe we need to find an object the killer is hoping to resurrect."

"That's brilliant, Grace."

"Thanks. Do you mind wrapping things up with Mizer? It's a big bust, for sure, and he's going to end up in jail. But if I don't strike right now, I fear—"

"Nope. Go on and do your thing. I'll do my best not to punch this one again."

"Well if you have a little slip-up, I promise not to tell anyone."

157

She raced back to the temporary office Palmer had been using and logged into the database with the log-in information he kept rather carelessly on a Post-It by the keyboard. She wasn't even quite sure what she was looking for as her fingers started trying keywords and search filters.

Females of Creole decent. Age range of twenty to twenty-five. Deaths within the last year.

There were far too many results to comb through. She tried narrowing the search down to women that had been murdered, as the case itself revolved around a ritual that was resulting in the deaths of these women.

The list was shortened, but as she quickly read through various reports, only a few fell into the parameters of what she was looking for. She jotted those case numbers down and tried narrowing the field again. This time she tried murders related to drug activity. The list grew even shorter, but none of the cases she found lined up.

Then, taking a long shot, she tried searching for deaths caused by car accidents. After all, aside from murder, which other form of death was so unpredictable, sudden, and tragic? What other form of death ripped life away so suddenly and harshly. One minute you're driving to get groceries, the next there's a terrible accident and someone in perfect health is suddenly no longer there.

Someone dipping into the well of black magic in trying to resurrect a lost loved one was surely the result of sudden earth-shattering tragedy. Maybe a car accident of some kind would be the sort of tragic event to push someone to such lengths.

Surprisingly, the result was only seven cases long based on her search filters.

And when she came to the second one, she felt her blood go cold.

For a moment, it was as if she were looking directly into the face of at least two of their victims. It wasn't a perfect match at all, but the resemblance was enough to cause a double-take. Change the hair, add some makeup, raise the eyes just a bit...yeah, it was DAMN close.

She scanned the report even as she was already giving the command for it to print out. Elisa Samberg, twenty-one years of age. She'd been killed when she'd started crossing a four-way intersection, truck at an angle by a drunk driver that had sped through a stop sign. She'd called her father first, and then an ambulance. She'd apparently lost an arm during the accident. From what she could tell from the report, her father had arrived first and taken her out of the car. He'd dragged her away from the ruins of the car and they'd collapsed together out in a field by the highway.

She was dead when the ambulance arrived. The father had passed out in shock, only to be brought back around and informed that his daughter had died.

And while all of that was certainly tragic enough, Camille's eyes went back to Elisa Samberg's face. She could still see the resemblance to the other victims.

She didn't know what it meant, exactly. But she did feel this could be the biggest lead so far. And if the broiling feeling in her guts was any indication, it might even lead to putting an end to this killer.

The question, of course, was how to predict where the killer would strike next. If he had a ritual in mind and was playing by some dark and evil rulebook, she would never be able to figure it out. It would be like shooting in the dark.

But as she got to her feet, the case file clutched in her hand, she realized that she knew someone who did.

And he was currently just down the hall in an interrogation room, bleeding and on the verge of going to jail for a very long time.

She hurried down the hallway and as she neared the door, she saw that same nervous-looking cop that had handed her Karen Henried's information.

"Agent! Agent Grace!"

"Yes?"

"We just got a call from a parking garage attendant out in the French Quarter. He says he saw something that raised some red flags. A man carrying an apparently comatose woman out of the parking garage. He says he checked over the security feeds and can see where the man sort of starts following the woman. Then they get on an elevator and that's it."

"What's the address of the parking garage?"

"I've already texted it to Agent Palmer."

"Excellent."

Camille stood where she was for a moment, torn on which avenue to follow up on. Then, still gripping the case file on Elisa Samberg's accident, she figured she could kill two birds with one stone.

With anger and a burning determination in her heart, Camille stepped back into the interrogation room, willing to do whatever it took to get the information out of him.

CHAPTER THIRTY THREE

"Mizer, let's not screw around here," Camille said. "You want the whole truth? Want us to come clean?"

He looked baffled for a moment. Palmer did, too, but there was interest in his stare. She thought it might actually be something slightly resembling amusement.

"Yes, we came to your house for another unrelated crime. But given the state of your house and what we found in the basement, we had every right to assume we were in the right place."

"So you messed up," he said with a bloodied grin. "I can go?"

"That's a huge no. There's a woman in the hospital that is in emaciated shape because of whatever fucked up ritual you were trying to conduct. But the case we are working on—the case that brought us to our home—is still active. And I just got a breakthrough that I need your help with. You can continue to be stubborn if you want, but it's only going to come out looking worse for you in the end."

Mizer pointed to his bloodied mouth and chin, laughing. "You think I'm going to help you after this?"

"I do. Because if you don't, I won't have a very hard time linking you to our current case, too. After what you did to that girl in your basement, the public won't have a hard time buying it. Four girls, Mizer. Five if you don't help us right now. If the public thinks we got the guy that did all of it, they'll just take us at our word. That's what people tend to do when they start to get scared. Given your line of work, I'm surprised you don't know that."

Having caught on to her approach, Palmer stepped forward with confidence. "Right now, we've got you on abduction and suspected rape of one woman. That's severe, but not quite as severe as having your hands in the deaths of five women."

Camille gave Mizer roughly two seconds to think this over before she slapped Elisa Samberg's file down on the table in front of him.

"This young woman was killed in a car accident several months ago. Our victims all look like her and we believe the killer is enacting rituals pertaining to either voodoo or black magic. They are stripped of their clothes, their necks are cut, and there is a pattern of little raised bumps between their breasts. Are you familiar with this set up?"

Mizer nodded curtly. "Yes. It is not too dissimilar from what I have tried to do."

"Is the killer trying to resurrect her?"

Mizer's eyes narrowed here. Camille thought he might sense that he had been trapped.

"Perhaps."

"Who would the killer have to come to in order to learn how to do something like that?"

Mizer simply looked to them, his eyes full of acknowledgement. "Who do you think? I am the only one with that sort of knowledge in this city."

"Do you...do you know who is doing this?"

"I believe so, yes. A man came to me not too long ago, wanting to know how to right a wrong the world had dished out to him."

"And what did you tell him?"

Mizer looked down at the file in front of him and then back up at the detectives, his teeth grinding. "I told him he was out of his mind."

"So you didn't help him?"

"I told him what needed to be done," he said. Slowly, a small wave of worry worked itself across his face. "I didn't think he'd honestly go through with it. I warned him."

"About what?" Palmer asked.

"I told him that there are consequences for everything. That it was not for him to correct the course of nature."

"Was this man's last name Samberg?" Camille asked.

"I don't know. I never ask for the names of people that come to me for help. I avoid personal connections."

"Fine. What did he look like?"

"Tall, dark hair, big-time muscles. He had glasses on though, so I might not be remembering him too accurately. He was quite sad. You could smell the sorrow on him, like rain."

"Listen to me," Camille said, again leaning again the table and looking down to him. "A fifth girl has been taken. We just got the call. It's very recent and we may be able to save her. If he is indeed trying to resurrect his daughter, where would he need to go?"

Mizer chuckled here again, but there was little humor in it. "Not the forest, that is for sure. People think there is power there, just because nature is so thick. So present."

"Then *where*?" Camille asked. "We don't have time to waste."

"You'll make sure it's noted that I assisted with this?" Mizer asked, grinning.

Palmer took a step forward and gave him a hard right-handed jab, right across the cheek.

"Yes, now we will," Palmer said.

Mizer groaned and when he looked back to the case file on the table, he spit on it. Blood-streaked phlegm washed across it. It took everything within Camille not to add her own jab.

"I didn't give him the instructions. Not the complete ones, because I thought he was an idiot. But perhaps he's figure it out on his own by now."

"Damn it, *where*?" Camille asked.

"To the place where she died. He must offer the new vessel in the location where his daughter's soul was taken."

Camille didn't even bother with a closing comment or confirming anything with Palmer. She simply turned and headed out of the door.

Seconds later, she sensed Palmer behind her. She also saw the eyes of about a dozen or so officers watching her with great interest as she tore through the precinct, to the front doors.

Palmer caught up to her just as she was reaching out for the first door.

"That intersection from the case file is half an hour away," he said. "If he got this girl fifteen or twenty minutes ago—"

"Then we'd better haul ass."

That said, the agents stepped out into the night, running for their car and, hopefully, an end to this killer's delusions.

***

Night had fallen, and Camille had to sit patiently in the passenger seat of the car while Palmer drove. She would have much preferred to drive, but Palmer knew the city better. His current understanding of the streets and avenues was a bit crisper than her own muddy memories of the city.

Palmer sped through the city, the red bubble light flashing along the dashboard of their sedan. Camille watched with a feverish anticipation as New Orleans glowed on the other side of the windows. It thinned out eventually, leading into the more rural area where the city became little more than a stretched out ray of light to the right.

162

She thought of the four girls that had already been killed. Heading like a rocket into the darker rural areas outside of the city, it was hard not to feel as if she was being escorted along by each of those young women, delivering them to the feet of their destroyer.

Camille closed her eyes, trying to imagine an aggrieved father that hurt so badly, so deeply, that he would resort to things like this. She tried to imagine what it was like to understand that his ritual had not worked and he was, at the core of it all, simply killing these women. What sort of heart-wrenching sorrow would drive a man to such things?

When she opened her eyes, she saw a stretch of blacktop ahead of them. There were tall trees to the right, and an open field to the left. They were rapidly approaching a vehicle that slowed and pulled to the side of the road to let them pass. Camille looked at the speedometer and saw that Palmer had the car gunned up to ninety.

"How much farther?" she asked.

"Five minutes at most." His eyes were glued dead ahead, his hands flexing tight around the steering wheel. They tore through the night like a bullet.

"Right there," Palmer said, his voice quick and stern. "Right up ahead."

Camille looked ahead and saw the intersection fast approaching. It looked desolate in the glow of the headlights. Even more alarming, there was a car pulled off to the side of the road just several feet away from the intersection. There were no doors open, nor anything hanging from the windows to indicate a breakdown.

Camille had no problem assuming it belonged to their killer.

Palmer brought their car to a stop, leaving the lights going and parking behind the abandoned car.

They stepped out of the car and found nothing. No body in the road, no presence of the killer. Nothing. There was only the car and the tall trees to all sides.

"Where the hell is he?" Palmer asked.

Camille looked to the car, walking over to it and peered in through the windows. It was spotless inside.

"Maybe we run the plates," she said. "Run the plates and—"

She stopped here as a thought occurred to her. She looked to her right, to the dark, dense thicket of trees. Mostly elms and large oaks, from what she could tell.

"Shit," she said, pulling her Glock. With it gripped in her hand, the forest beside her seemed darker somehow. It was a darkness that

163

invited her in, trying to remind her that as a girl, she'd explored forests like these, not too far from here.

"What is it?" Palmer asked.

"Mizer said the killer would go to where the daughter died," she said. "And she didn't die here on the road. She was pronounced dead when the medics found her."

She looked to the little strip of grass that separated the road from the trees. It was only about twenty feet or so but in that moment, it looked about as wide as a sea.

"And they found her out there."

Palmer nodded and together, they ran away from the road and into the thick and waiting darkness ahead.

CHAPTER THIRTY FOUR

The strip of land between the road and the tree line was unremarkable, but Camille still nearly fell on two occasions. Once, when she tripped over a thick clump of tangled weeds and again when she had to sidestep a tree branch that had been lurking in the tall grass and the darkness.

A small beam of light appeared from her right as Palmer had the good sense to pull out a small flashlight and point it in the direction of the trees.

When they arrived there, she could still see no sign of the killer. She went back through the details of the report in her mind. The young woman's left arm had been severed in the accident. The father arrived before the ambulance and helped her out of the car. He'd dragged her off to the right and that's where the medics found them.

The report had not said WHERE though.

She scanned the darkness, her eyes dancing along the thick and tangled of trees and their branches. The forest was thick and dark, alive with the singing of insects.

The area by the tree line was in absolute darkness, a black hole into which Palmer had to point their beams of light to get any kind of vision at all. It was difficult to come close to the edge without tripping over debris, thick roots and rocks that jutted up from the ground like the teeth of some primeval monster waiting to be fed.

She walked a few steps into the brush, each foot causing a small rustling sound in the tall weeds.

And then, between steps, she heard the sound of a man's weeping.

She turned to the left and saw a figure against a tree. It was so dark that she almost missed it, but the shape of a human shoulder sticking out from the tree clued her in. She reached out to Palmer and turned him slightly so that his light went in that direction.

With another step forward, they saw him.

A man stood, slightly bowed, by the base of a large tree. There was a girl on the ground at his feet, propped against the trunk. She had been stripped naked and her head was propped over to the side, almost resting on her left shoulder.

It was hard to be certain because of the darkness and shadows, but Camille was pretty sure her neck had not yet been sliced.

She looked back to the man and saw the knife in his hand, glinting like a harsh secret by Palmer's flashlight.

"Mr. Samberg?" Camille said.

He didn't bother turning around. In fact, he did not respond at all. Camille figured he'd known they were here from the moment they arrived. That pulsing red light on the dashboard would have been a hard to miss even while standing in this thicket of trees.

"Mr. Samberg, I need you to step away from the girl and drop the knife."

Without turning to them, Samberg said: "It's not going to work. I should have always known. This is my last chance and I still feel that I didn't do something right."

Camille stepped forward a bit more, her hand still tight around the Glock.

"It's not too late to do the right thing," Camille said. "I can't imagine the pain you felt when she died, but you have to know deep down that this won't work. You can't undo it."

He finally turned. He did so very quickly, so fast that Camille was certain he was about to come charging at her. She felt her trigger beneath her finger, ready to squeeze if she needed to.

"She didn't deserve to die. I can bring her back. I just need to get the ritual right. I need to..."

He was crying as he spoke, and each word came from his mouth without much conviction. Camille felt pity for him because she didn't think he truly believed the things he was saying. He'd lost himself to grief, to the sorrow of losing his daughter. She doubted he even understood the severity of the things he'd done, and what he was about to do to this fifth woman.

"Mr. Samberg, we can talk about this," Camille said. "We can figure a way out. But I need you to drop that knife."

"I can't. I have to try."

"You know this won't work. Deep down, sir, don't you KNOW it? Even if this act of darkness does work, do you really think the thing that comes to fill this body will try be your daughter?"

Samberg's face scrunched up into a look of agony. "I don't...I don't know. But I have to try. I'm sorry. I'm sorry."

His voice had gone higher, but not in the manner of a man on the verge of hysterics. It was the voice of a man pleading, begging for

166

forgiveness. He was crying without shame. She could see the tears on his face and his shoulders shaking.

"Mr. Samberg, please. I need you to drop the knife."

"No. I have to try. I have to."

He started to lower himself down into what looked to be a kneeling position. He moved slowly, sobbing and trembling as he moved.

Not taking her eyes away from Samberg, she whispered to Palmer. "When he looks up, shine the light in his eyes."

Palmer nodded, his eyes also locked on Samberg.

"Mr. Samberg, this is your last warning," she said. And then, raising her voice and injecting bass into it, she said. "Look at me, sir! Give me just one more second of your time."

"I have to do this," he moaned. But he did turn to look at her.

And when he did, Palmer shined the light up into the man's eyes.

Samberg winced and flinched back, bringing his free hand up to block the light. He stumbled back a bit in surprise.

By the time his hand was blocking the light, Camille was already charging forward.

It took only three huge steps to reach him and when she did, she grabbed his right wrist as she also threw her right shoulder into his chest. They both went sprawling backwards against the tree. Samberg's back slammed into it and the knife went flying from his hand. Yet at about the same time, he threw a quick elbow back and caught Camille in the chest.

The pain dropped her to a knee and before she was fully aware of what was happening, he fell on top of her. She felt his hands reaching for her throat, scrambling for purchase, trying to choke her. But as he did his best to perch himself on top of her, she straightened out her right leg and brought it up hard. It not only caught him in the crotch, but she also slipped him up and over.

When he hit the ground, Palmer was there with handcuffs out and waiting. When he brought Samberg's arms around behind him, the man attempted to fight back, but he was just too emotionally drained. When he tried to spring a fist out to take Palmer in the ribs, he sidestepped it easily. Camille caught Samberg's arm following the missed blow and yanked it up behind him, spinning him around. Palmer applied the cuffs and pressed him hard against the tree.

"No!" Samberg yelled. "You have to let me try! I have to at least *try!*"

Palmer pulled out his cellphone and called for an ambulance. He hunkered down in front of the woman as he did so. He lifted her arm to check her pulse and after a few moments, at about the same time he started speaking into the phone, he gave Camille a thumbs up.

The woman was alive.

Samberg began to wail and scream on the ground. It wasn't the sound of anger or defeat, but of acceptance. His daughter was gone, and she was not coming back and in coming to terms with that, he'd taken four innocent lives.

Had Camille not seen the faces of those four dead women, she may have pitied him a bit more.

But as it was, all she could muster for him was a pained indifference as they stood beneath the night sky and the canopy of trees, waiting for the ambulance to arrive.

CHAPTER THIRTY FIVE

Camille did her best to spruce up the stagnant police station coffee, but it still tasted bitter and very much like reheated, police station coffee. She took two sips and dumped it down the sink.

It wasn't like she needed it. She hadn't slept in nearly two days. She fully intended to finally get the hotel room she should have gotten the night before and sleep for about ten hours before heading back home.

The interrogation of Luis Samberg took less than forty minutes. He confessed to all four murders and even told them where he'd acquired each one. He explained the ritual and though it seemed like a lot of dark nonsense to Camille, it was chilling nonetheless.

As she gathered her thoughts and watched the very bad coffee go swirling down the drain, Palmer entered the little break room. He looked just as tired as she was, but there had been a considerable shift in his mood ever since both Luis Samberg and the fifth woman had been removed from the site by the side of the road.

"Anyone ever tell you that you're kind of amazing at your job?" Palmer asked.

"A few."

"I'm not going to lie: I wish you were a permanent fixture here. It was nice to have someone to bounce ideas off of."

"Even though I snapped at you about asking about my past?"

Palmer shrugged. "I get it. I have things in my past I'd rather not dredge up, too. As far as I'm concerned, all is forgiven."

"Likewise. And you're pretty good at your job, too."

He grinned. "I know. Anyway, I did get Mizer to confirm one of the details Samberg told us. The little bumps around the chest are all making a pattern. It's different for each girl, the pattern alternating every time he uses it. It's supposed to represent the symbol for eternal life in some obscure voodoo practices and dark magic circles."

"He hadn't put them on the girl from tonight, though."

"Yeah, I noticed that, too."

Camille thought about the other girl. All she knew for sure was that she was in stable condition in an ICU ward. She'd gotten no update on whether or not she had indeed been raped as Mizer had claimed, but she wasn't sure she even wanted to know.

"So what's next for you?" Camille asked.

"Wrapping up things with Mizer, I suppose. I'm sure some hard, constant interrogation is going to reveal a lot more depraved acts."

"Keep me in the loop on that, would you? Maybe there's some report-work I can assist with."

"That's a deal." He hesitated for a moment and then stepped further into the room. "Look. I know it's late as hell, but do you think you'd be up for a drink?"

She eyed him skeptically for a moment, wondering if she was being set up for a joke. It seemed completely senseless to her that he'd be asking her out.

"Now?" she said.

"Yeah. Now."

Camille glanced at her watch. Not that she needed to. She knew right away she was going to decline. Not because she didn't want to spend the extra time with Palmer, but because she was too damned exhausted. "I can't. I need to find a hotel and crash. I'm absolutely wiped out."

"Tomorrow?"

She smiled and shrugged. "I don't know. Can we just see how tomorrow goes?"

He smiled right back and shook his head. "No, that's okay. I can handle the subtle rejections better than the flat out kind."

"That's not a total rejection. I'm legitimately wiped out."

"I know. I can see that. But I'll tell you what. If you're ever back in town, drinks are on me."

She offered her hand to him and he took it, not looking away from her eyes.

"I'm going to hold you to that, Agent Palmer."

They held one another's gaze for a few seconds before Camille left the room. As she passed down the hallway, she looked to the closed door of the interrogation room Luis Samberg was occupying. She knew she'd have to write up field notes and reports, but that could wait until after a good night's sleep.

Besides, after that, she had one more stop to make before she returned to Alabama.

***

170

It was shortly after eight o' clock in the morning when Camille turned her borrowed precinct car down Deanna Lewiston's driveway. Revisiting Deanna now that the case was closed felt a little less stressful. Now, it was more like visiting a dear old friend than a means of clearing her head and escaping the madness of the case.

As she brought the car to a stop, she saw Deanna sitting in a rocking chair on the front porch. A coffee mug was sitting on a small overturned barrel used as a table, and a book sat in her lap.

When Camille stepped out of the car, she took a moment to breathe in the morning. Here, in the woods of Upping, New Orleans could be half a world away. She smelled pines, spruces, and the ever-so-faint aroma of the swamplands that began a little less than ten miles away.

It felt like home and though it unnerved her a bit, she was willing to admit that there was something comforting about it, too.

"I was wondering if you'd come back by," Deanna called out from the porch.

"Yeah, sorry about yesterday. It was one hell of a day. One hell of a case."

"You don't have to explain yourself or apologize. Come on up and have some coffee, would you?"

Camille walked up the stairs and was surprised to see that the book on Deanna's lap was a King James Bible. She could remember nothing from her childhood years around Deanna that indicated she'd been a religious woman.

Deanna apparently noticed her glance of confusion. She placed the little ribbon bookmark across the pages, and shrugged.

"I'm not one of those holy rollers, if that's what you're thinking."

"That's not what I was thinking. But…well, am I interrupting something?"

"No, not at all. I just find it easier to concentrate out here." She tapped the Bible and sighed. "The urge hit me out of nowhere a few years ago. There's so much meanness in the world. I needed to find something to give me some hope. I tried meditation but don't have the focus or discipline for it."

Camille grinned and said, "And Christianity doesn't require either of those?"

Deanna laughed and said, "Not so much, now that I've read a lot of it.

"What are you looking for in there?"

"I don't know. Maybe answers. Why did the world become the way it is? Why do human beings have to hurt each other? If there's a God, why won't he come down and stop it?"

Camille shrugged and thought of how Luis Samberg had been so tormented over trying to fight against the evil desires inside of himself. How, even with four already dead and his moral compass certainly fractured, he *knew* what he was doing was wrong.

"Maybe he has," Camille said. "Maybe he has and we're just too stupid to see it."

Deanna considered this for a moment and then got to her feet. "I'll get you some coffee. One second."

There was no second chair on the porch, so Camille simply stood. She looked out to the forest and could not help but wonder what other sort of crimes and atrocities took place out there. As a child, this same stretch of forest had been a place of wonder, discovery, and imagined adventures. Eyeing them with the filter of an experienced FBI agent having come off of a brutal case was quite a different experience.

Deanna came back out with a cup of aromatic coffee. Camille sipped from it and found it just about perfect.

"You're going to have to forgive me," Deanna said. "But I have to ask: do you plan on going to see your father?"

"No." The answer came quickly and easily.

"And...I guess you heard about your mother?"

"I don't want to hear about my mother."

"She's dead, Camille. She died three years ago. Found dead in a hotel room down in Texas."

Camille sensed something broken in her when she could not muster up a single shred of emotion over this news. While her mother had essentially been dead to her for about twenty years now, it *should* have been different o have confirmation that the woman really was dead.

"Your father didn't want to reach out and tell you and I had no idea how to get in touch with you. You never really left any means for anyone to get in touch with you when you left Upping."

"That was intentional."

"Yet here you are, visiting me."

"Yeah," Camille said. "I guess I am."

Deanna took a sip of her own coffee and gave Camille a blank stare. Camille couldn't deduce the woman's thoughts from her expression.

172

"Why are you here?" she asked. "The last time I saw you, you were heading to college. Then I heard you were heading to Quantico. Then nothing. So I'm just hoping you're not coming to tell me you're off on some other grand adventure. Not getting on a fishing boat to go to Alaska or something like that."

"No. I was just in New Orleans for this case. I felt Upping looming over me like a shadow and knew I had to at least visit. And when I pulled that trigger, I wanted to come see you."

"How did you know I hadn't moved or something?"

"You're too much of a homebody. You love the area too much."

Deanna grinned guiltily. "Yeah, I do."

"How have you been, D?"

"Can't complain. Remember the birdhouses I built all the time?"

"I do," Camille said, smiling. Looking out into the yard, she saw two of them situated along the eastern side of the yard.

"This young man down at the library helped me set up an Etsy shop. You know Etsy?"

Camille nodded, drinking from her coffee.

"I've been making and selling birdhouses on there for the last four years. I'm making about three times as much as I ever did down at the stupid post office."

"That's great to hear."

There was an awkward paused between them, the sort of pause that Camille could sense had something heavy on the other end of it.

"You need to go see him," Deanna said.

"I haven't forgiven him yet."

"It doesn't matter. Camille...he's sick. We aren't sure what it is just yet because he's stubborn and won't go to a specialist. But right now, we don't know what it is or how bad it is."

Camille looked to the right, to the trees, over their jagged tops. Her father's house was over there, about six miles away.

"No. Not yet."

"Then when?"

"Can we just enjoy our coffee?" Camille said. "Deanna...you know what he did. And you know just as well as I do that he probably deserves to still be in prison."

"I know. And no...I haven't forgotten." She grinned and laid her hands on the closed Bible. "But I'm starting to learn a bit about forgiveness."

"Yeah, well, I haven't."

173

She left it at that and tore her eyes away from the trees.

"Please don't tell me you came by to visit and this is how things are going to go."

Camille shook her head. "They don't have to. Come on. Can you show me your Etsy shop? And maybe sell me a birdhouse?"

"Now we're talking."

Together, they walked inside. For the briefest of moments, as Camille passed through the doorway with Deanna in front of her, she felt like a child again. Then all of childhood rose up in front of her, overshadowing her adult self for just a moment. There was relief and solitude here at Deanna's while the specter of her father flitted about over both of them.

It truly *was* similar to when she was a child. Only now, there was a very mature bitterness in Camille's heart. And not even the warm, familiar corners and nooks of Deanna's house calling out from her childhood memories, could break through it.

CHAPTER THIRTY SIX

Camille returned home at 9:45 that night. She stepped through the lobby doors, took the elevator up to her third floor apartment, but then stopped in front of her door.

Why did this not feel like home?

When she slid her key into the lock, why was she thinking of the fragmented treetops that looked down over the small, rural nothing that was Upping?

Why was she thinking of Deanna sitting on her porch, sipping coffee and reading from her Bible.

She turned they key and walked inside.

Declan was sitting on the couch, watching a detective show and eating pizza. He'd gotten delivery again, the box sitting on the coffee table, which was littered with his laptop and a few empty beer cans. The apartment had a stale smell that was almost like a locker room. Not really sweaty but very *human*.

Declan turned to look at her and offered a smile that took very little effort. He did not get up to hug her, comforted by the fact that she was back, that she had made it through a case that had offered up dangerous situations at every turn.

No, he gave her a lazy smile and turned back to the television as he slid a slice of pizza into his mouth.

"You crack the case?" he asked as he chewed.

"I did. What have you been doing the last three days?"

"Not much."

He wasn't even trying to act as if he had any purpose any longer. She wondered if he'd applied for jobs while she'd been gone. She also wondered how much PlayStation he'd played, how much TV he'd consumed.

"I can see that."

She ventured into the kitchen and saw a mess of dishes piled in the sink. The garbage can, while not overflowing, was emitting an unpleasant smell.

She thought of the smell of the distant swamplands. She thought of driving through Upping. She thought of her father, of all things.

"I know what you are now…why'd you have to be so good?

She'd never heard her father's voice so clearly in her mind while being so far-removed from Upping. It nearly took her breath.

"Declan?" she said.

"Yeah, babe." He still wasn't looking at her. She figured he would when the show was off, and he was wanting sex. It had been three days, after all.

"Do you even want to do this? This relationship. Me and you?" There was no emotion to it. She may as well have been standing in a courtroom, talking to a jury.

"Oh, so we're doing this again? Already?"

"Yes. We are."

"Fine." He made a very big, dramatic deal about turning the TV off and then tossed the remote to the other end of the couch.

"You're serious about this? You're going to start with this again? Really?"

"I am."

"Why?"

"Because I deserve better than this, Declan."

"You mean you deserve better than *me*, don't you?"

"Yes. I'll admit that. If you don't do something to change the way you're living, yes. That's a fair statement."

"We've done this, Camille. We've been over this. I love you. I want to be with you."

"Do you?" she asked.

"Yes."

"Love me?"

"Yes."

"No, I don't think you do, Declan. I think you like me. I think you tolerate being around me. You like the idea of a girlfriend, and you like the sex. You like that an attractive, educated woman would fall for your charms and the things you say. You like the idea of me paying for everything, of me being your meal ticket."

He looked speechless for a moment and then sneered at her. He pointed an accusing finger her way and said, "You're getting a big head over this Sir Richard arrest. You're not as big of a deal as you think. So what if you busted that guy? That's your job. Congratulations for doing *your job*. It doesn't give you the right to lord yourself over me."

176

The number of rebuttals that came to mind were too many to count. Rather than stand there and try to decide on one, she went into the bedroom.

"Good talk," Declan called out from the living room.

Camille let the comment sail right over her head. She ignored it as she opened the closet and searched around for the small suitcase she sometimes took on trips she knew would take a week or more. She found it in the back and tossed it on the bed.

She then took several minutes to throw some clothes and other essentials into the suitcase. It felt liberating and a bit frightening.

But it was also what needed to be done.

The man sitting on the couch in the living room was one of the many reasons this place no longer felt like home.

But she was also not naive enough to lay it all at his feet. She'd been mostly fine staying here before the trip to New Orleans. Before the trip back to Upping.

She packed quickly, not wanting to give Declan the chance to come in and confront her. Not that she really thought he would.

She finished packing as she tossed her spare toothbrush in on top of a few changes of clothes. She zipped the case and hefted it off the bed onto the floor. She took a moment to look at the bed, to imagine herself and Declan there. They'd had some good days near the start of their relationship; there had been entire weekend when they rarely left the bedroom.

But that was gone now, part of another life.

She apparently had lots of those other lives...her family consisting of one of them. Her father. Her mother. Nannette, her missing and probably dead sister.

She carried the suitcase through the hallway, the kitchen, and finally into the living room. When Declan saw what was happening, he sat up quickly.

"You're kidding, right?"

"I'm not. I'm leaving, Declan. There's no point in my staying here."

"You can't just leave. It's *your* place."

"Actually, it's *our* place. Remember? I put you down as a resident a few months ago when you quit your job...so it would look good on job applications."

"Come on, Camille. We can work through this."

"You're right. And that's what I'm doing. And part of me working through it is leaving you. Maybe finding a home somewhere else."

"You...you're talking crazy."

She laughed unironically as she headed for the door. "You know...maybe I am." And then, because she couldn't help but get in the last word against a man that had gotten so many of them in during the last year or so, she added: "You need to send the rent to the landlord by the fifteenth of each month."

That was the last thing she said before making her way out. When the door was closed behind her, she heard him yell out a curse, but he never came after her.

She made her way back down to the lobby and out to her car. She sat there for a while, not quite sure where she'd go. A hotel for now. Just until she got her bearings straight.

Maybe until she could get a better grip on what she thought HOME was supposed to feel like.

She thought of Upping and even of the busier and well-known parts of New Orleans. Was home a place that was familiar and reassuring, or was it where you went to feel safe?

She didn't know.

And either way, she wasn't sure she knew of any place that did that for her.

She supposed it was about time she found out. Even if that meant looking deeper into her heartbreaking past, she had to find the answer.

And she also thought there was a very good possibility that it would start with taking a long, hard look at her sister's case.

Any answers to her past would be hidden there. And she'd purposefully never bothered to look.

Pushed by a newfound purpose, excitement, and a healthy dose of fear, Camille pulled out into the street, looking for home.

NOW AVAILABLE!

NOT NOW
(A Camille Grace FBI Suspense Thriller—Book 2)

In this new series by #1 bestselling—and critically-acclaimed—mystery and suspense author Kate Bold, Camille Grace, a rising star in the FBI's BAU unit, is dispatched to the one place she vowed to never return: the deep South. When bodies turn up in the swamps, victims of alligator attacks, something seems awry, and Camille must discover if this is mother nature—or the work of a new serial killer.

"Phenomenal debut with a huge creep factor… So many twists and turns, you'll have no idea who the next victim will be. If you love a thriller that will keep you awake well into the night, this book is for you."
—Reader review for *Let Me Go*

Camille clashes with her partner, convinced there is more to the deaths than alligator attacks—and yet she, herself, is puzzled: who would commit such a twisted crime? Why?

At the same time, Camille feels compelled to dive back into her sister's cold case, and into the disappearance that has haunted her for her entire life. Might she find a new lead?

First, though, she must race a ticking clock to save the next victim in time.

Unless the killer finds her first.

A riveting psychological crime thriller full of mystery and suspense, the CAMILLE GRACE mystery series will make you fall in love with a brilliant new female protagonist. Packed with twists and turns, her story will keep you flipping pages late into the night.

The series begins with NOT ME (book #1), and book #3 in the series (NOT WELL) is now also available.

"This is an excellent book... When you start reading, be sure you don't have to wake up early!"
—Reader review for The Killing Game

"I really enjoyed this book... It draws you in right away and keeps you turning the pages right up to the end. I am really anticipating the next book."
—Reader review for Let Me Go

"WOW what a great read! Talk about a diabolical killer! Really enjoyed this book. Looking forward to reading others by this author as well."
—Reader review for The Killing Game

"Excellent start to a new series... Get this book and read it, you will love it!"
—Reader review for Let Me Go

"Captivating and riveting serial murder with a twist of the macabre... Very well done."
—Reader review for The Killing Game

"Good read with good plot, plenty of action, and great character development. A thriller that will keep you awake into the night."
—Reader review for Let Me Go

Kate Bold

Debut author Kate Bold is author of the ALEXA CHASE SUSPENSE THRILLER series, comprising six books (and counting); the ASHLEY HOPE SUSPENSE THRILLER series, comprising six books (and counting); and the CAMILLE GRACE FBI SUSPENSE THRILLER series, comprising three books (and counting).

An avid reader and lifelong fan of the mystery and thriller genres, Kate loves to hear from you, so please feel free to visit www.kateboldauthor.com to learn more and stay in touch.

BOOKS BY KATE BOLD

ALEXA CHASE SUSPENSE THRILLER
THE KILLING GAME (Book #1)
THE KILLING TIDE (Book #2)
THE KILLING HOUR (Book #3)
THE KILLING POINT (Book #4)
THE KILLING FOG (Book #5)
THE KILLING PLACE (Book #6)

ASHLEY HOPE SUSPENSE THRILLER
LET ME GO (Book #1)
LET ME OUT (Book #2)
LET ME LIVE (Book #3)
LET ME BREATHE (Book #4)
LET ME FORGET (Book #5)
LET ME ESCAPE (Book #6)

CAMILLE GRACE FBI SUSPENSE THRILLER
NOT ME (Book #1)
NOT NOW (Book #2)
NOT WELL (Book #3)

9 781094 394428